# The Takeover Episodes 1-4

## The Takeover

Jasmine Bishop

Published by Heartness Crane Publishing, 2023.

THE TAKEOVER EPISODES 1-4

**First edition. August 23, 2023.**

ISBN: 979-8223163978

Written by Jasmine Bishop.

Amanda stood a few yards away from the entrance to the Obsidian Lounge and took a moment to compose herself. It was still early, and the underground parking lot hadn't yet filled up.

She smiled as a group of well-dressed women held their phones out to be scanned. Ivy, dark hair tucked into her white beret, a walkie on her hip, beeped them in and wished them a good evening. Once they were all inside, Amanda adjusted her purse and approached the station.

Ivy was fashionably dressed in a crisp white shirt and black skirt. She looked up from her clipboard and smiled in recognition. "Amanda! What is it tonight, business or pleasure? Are you here for a meeting with Miss Starr?"

"Business, I guess. Apparently, I'm training tonight."

Ivy's eyes lit up. "Shut up! You're working here now? What did we do to get so lucky?"

Amanda shrugged. "Erica wants me to get some experience working here. For the book."

"For the book, sure." Ivy gave her a subtle wink. "I'll bet you tried real hard to get out of it."

"I'm kind of nervous, actually. I've never really danced before."

"Never?" Ivy twirled a lock of black hair around on her finger and flipped it back. "Not even once?"

*Is she flirting with me? Because I like it. Why did I never notice how cute she is before?*

"Not like this. Not at a real club."

"And not just any club." Ivy raised her arm and pointed at the neon sign of them. "Only a special class of ladies dance at the Obsidian Lounge. Miss Starr has high standards, you know."

"Thanks. That makes me feel so much better."

"Oh, don't worry, Amanda. You're going to be great. You're totally hot. The women will love you, and I'll bet you walk out of here with a ton of tips. No problem at all." Ivy paused. "Wait a minute. Where's your outfit?"

"Outfit?" Amanda thought for a moment. "Oh, shit."

Ivy laughed. "Erica really sent you down here without a change of clothes?" She shook her head. "A fashionable woman like her should really know better."

"See? I don't know what I'm doing."

"Oh, I'm sure the girls will help you out." She looked Amanda up and down and nodded her head. "They'll just wind up on the stage floor, anyway. Go on, get in there and have fun. Tell me all about it later, okay?"

"Sure, I'll give you the damage report."

"I'm off in an hour when the next girl gets here. I'll come inside and look for you." She gave a flirtatious smile. "I'll come sit at your stage and cheer you on."

Amanda smiled back. "I'd like that. It'll be nice to see a familiar face."

"You're going to be great." Ivy held the door open and waved her inside. "I'll see you later."

The evening was just getting started. Amanda had never been to the Lounge so early, and it looked brighter than the two times she'd been before. Most of the tables were still empty, but she knew they wouldn't be for long.

She walked past the main stage, where two women took turns spinning around the pole. She didn't know either of them, but recognized the bartender, Simone, and made her way to the bar.

"Excuse me, could you tell me how to get to the dressing room?" she asked.

Simone finished pouring a drink and set it in front of a woman with short, dark hair. "Hey, Amanda. What's up? Vivian asked me to keep an eye out for you. Sure. You've been to the Element Rooms before, right?"

Amanda nodded. "Yeah, I've been to the Water Room."

"Ooh, I love the Water Room." She pointed across the bar. "Take a right instead of going straight down the hall. Just follow the voices. They're all back there."

"I'll find it. Thank you, Simone."

"Of course. Have fun tonight and let me know if you need anything. I'll be here all night." Simone picked up a bottle of vodka and began mixing more drinks.

Amanda made her way past the rear stage. A gorgeous, dark-haired dancer slid effortlessly down the pole to a round of applause.

*There's no way I could do that. They'd laugh me right off the stage. Why did I agree to this?*

She stopped, took a deep breath, and prepared the same mental pep talk she gave herself before a busy restaurant shift.

*No. Don't indulge in negative thoughts. It's a skill like anything else. It can be learned. I can learn this.*

She calmed down a bit and smiled as she continued across the room.

*Okay, you've got this.*

Simone was right. A clamor of female voices arose from behind a bright red door. She knocked hesitantly. When the door opened, a familiar face greeted her.

"Hey, Sapphire," Amanda said. "I'm not late, am I?"

Sapphire pulled her in and gave her a warm hug. "Nope, you're right on time. We're going to have so much fun tonight, Amanda. I don't go on for half an hour, so there's plenty of time to show you around. Have you come up with a stage name yet?"

"I hadn't even thought about it." Amanda sighed. "I'm so not prepared for this."

"Sure you are. Let me introduce you to Ophelia and we can ask her. She's the queen of coming up with stage names." She put her arm around Amanda's shoulder and led her into the room.

There were a half-dozen ladies backstage in various stages of undress. A few walked around topless and unconcerned. A cute girl with short, fire-engine red hair sat at a table, struggling to put on a pair of white boots. When she saw Sapphire and Amanda, she stopped and smiled at them.

"Meet Amanda," Sapphire said. "She's new and needs to come up with a stage name. What do you think? Can you help her?"

Ophelia finished tying her laces and stood up. She was shorter than them both and wore a bright red metallic top and a short black skirt. "You have such amazing hair. I'm Ophelia."

"Hi," Amanda said. "Thank you."

"Hmm. Let me look at you." As Ophelia's eyes wandered up and down Amanda's body, she felt the unfamiliar sensation of being watched. A buzz of excitement built in her stomach, and she tensed up involuntarily before forcing herself to relax.

*When I'm on stage, everyone's going to be checking me out. I'd better get used to it now.*

"Once I find your essence, this will be easy," Ophelia said.

"My essence?"

"Yeah, you know. Your soul or whatever. Your essential nature, the part that makes you you."

Sapphire ran her hand along Amanda's arm. "Trust her. It's goofy, but she always figures it out. Every time."

Amanda looked around the room at a half-dozen women applying make-up and putting on their outfits. "I feel so plain around all of you."

"Bullshit," Ophelia said. "You're beautiful, and you have a strong soul essence."

"I do?"

"Yes, I can feel it. I think you're going to be a natural on stage." She looked at Amanda again. "Let's find a name for you. I'll go with my tried-and-true method."

"This one actually works most of the time," Sapphire said. "You'd be surprised."

"Go for it," Amanda said. "I'm ready."

"What was your best friend in middle school's name?"

"Maddy. Madeline."

Ophelia thought for a moment. "Nope. Not feeling it." She smiled. "Don't worry, there's another one. How about your grandmother's middle name?"

"Which one?"

"Your mom's mom."

"Pam. Pamela."

Ophelia scrunched her nose. "That's not any better. Tell you what, I'll keep at it and come up with one by the end of the night. Promise."

"Maybe watching her on stage will give you an idea," Sapphire said.

"I'm into it." Ophelia winked at Amanda flirtatiously. "I can already tell you're going to be fun once you loosen up."

Sapphire turned to Amanda. "All right, what did Erica send you here with? Where's your bag, and what amazing outfits did you bring tonight?"

Amanda cringed. "I didn't bring any."

"Amanda. You thought you'd just get up on stage in your street clothes?" Sapphire shook her head. "What were you thinking, girl?"

"It was all so sudden. Erica just told me I was coming down. I didn't have time to prepare, and nobody said anything about clothes."

Sapphire laughed. "Epic fail, girl. Lucky for you, I've got something you can wear tonight. But you'll need to buy a few outfits when this becomes a regular thing. We'll go shopping sometime. It'll be fun."

"I'm down for that. And I know just the place to go." Amanda thought back to her last shopping trip and the good time she'd had in the dressing room.

*We'll go visit Ruth. I wonder if her store's still open. I'll call her tomorrow and see how she's doing.*

Sapphire held out her hand and led Amanda to the back of the room. She browsed through a clothes-rack and brought down a low-cut white shirt and a short black skirt. "They're kind of basic, but they'll get you through the night."

She handed them to Amanda. "I think they'll fit, too. Go on, try them on."

"Right here?"

Sapphire looked at her. "Now, Amanda, when have you ever been modest? Yes, right here." She swatted her ass playfully. "I mean, I can turn my head if you want. But look around you."

Amanda laughed. "I see your point."

Sapphire looked at the clock. "Twenty minutes until I go on. Go ahead and get dressed. We'll sit at the stage and I can give you a few pointers. How much cash did you bring?"

"All I brought is my card," Amanda said as she took off her pants and slipped into the skirt. "I didn't think I'd need cash."

Sapphire shook her head. "How did you think we were going to tip the girls? Come on, you can buy me a drink and we'll get cash back from Simone."

"Oh, I'm buying your drinks now? I see how it is."

Sapphire smiled. "Girl, the education you'll get tonight will be priceless. Well worth a couple of vodka-7s."

Amanda laughed. "I believe it." She wrapped her arm around Sapphire. "Come on, let's go."

"You found her," Simone said as set four shots of tequila on a tray. She passed the tray to a server and turned to them.

"She sure did." Sapphire wrapped her arm around Amanda's shoulders. "I'm showing her around a bit before she makes her stage debut."

Amanda set her card on the bar and slid it forward.

"What are you having?" Simone asked.

"Vodka-7s?" Amanda asked Sapphire.

"Sounds great. And a hundred in fives back, please." She slid her hand down Amanda's back. "Is that okay?"

Amanda nodded. As Simone turned to mix their drinks, Sapphire let her hand linger on the small of Amanda's back. More than just sensual, the touch comforted and grounded her. For the first time that night, she felt like everything was going to be all right.

"Okay, ready for you first lesson? Get in good with the bartenders. They're your best friends in this place. Tip well, be patient, and always thank them." Sapphire slowly moved her hand away as their drinks arrived. "Oh, I forgot. You used to be a server. You get it."

Amanda nodded and sipped her drink. "Yeah, it's pretty easy to not be a jerk. Besides, I believe in karma."

Sapphire laughed. "Oh, you sound like Ophelia now. You two are going to have so much to talk about."

"I'm not a New Ager or anything like that." Amanda pulled a five off the stack of bills, set in on the bar, and put the rest in her pocket. "Really."

"Whatever you say, love." Sapphire looked toward the stage. "Look, she's up now. Let's go cheer her on."

She led Amanda across the floor and they found two empty seats at the corner of the stage. A group of three women sat in front, drinks and tips cluttering the rack. A dark-haired woman sat by herself on the other end.

Ophelia slid her legs around the pole, doing three complete spins, before walking over to the group of women.

"Always have some cash in front of you when you're at the stage," Sapphire told her. "Otherwise, all you're doing is taking space away from a paying customer." She took a sip of her drink. "Watch her. See how she flirts with patrons, how she uses her body and her mind. You can learn a lot from Ophelia if you pay attention."

Ophelia pressed herself against one of the women, draping her leg across the stage and running her hands up her thighs. Her skirt flipped up, and she gave the crowd a quick flash. Amanda noticed she wasn't wearing underwear and smiled to herself.

Sapphire pointed. "You see? Pure artistry." She leaned in and whispered in Amanda's ear. "One of those ladies is getting a dance tonight. You just wait."

Ophelia stood up and slid a pile of bills to the center of the stage with her foot. She walked across and leaned in to Sapphire. "Nice of you two to drop by. Are you enjoying the show?"

"I wanted Amanda to see how a class act does it before we get up there."

Ophelia laughed and slid over to Amanda. She teased her nipples and leaned down. "You know I just make this up as I go along, right? Just be yourself."

"That's all I do," Sapphire agreed.

"Don't worry about getting the moves down. They'll come with time." Ophelia pressed herself against Amanda's chest and slowly peeled away. "Just be open and friendly. It goes a long way."

Sapphire nodded and took a sip of her drink. "Listen to this girl. She knows what she's talking about."

"You ready to take it to the stage?" Ophelia nodded her head toward the group of women on the other side of the stage. "I'll come back and watch after I take care of this private dance."

"You'd better." Sapphire turned to Amanda. "We like to hype each other up around here, you know."

The music faded, and the next song came on. As Ophelia gathered her tips and clothes from the stage, she talked to one of the women for a moment, then hopped off stage. They walked toward the back room, arms around each other.

"Watch my purse," Sapphire said. "It's time for your next lesson. Put a five down in front of you." She winked. "I'll come back for it in a minute."

Sapphire climbed to the top of the pole. "Check this out," she called, twirling down with one leg. She landed on her feet gracefully, and Amanda clapped loudly along with the rest of the audience.

Sapphire made her way to the woman by herself in the corner. Her dark hair was cut short, and she wore a navy pantsuit. They talked for a few moments before Sapphire leaned in and gently rubbed herself on the woman.

*She's such a cute lady, but why does she seem out of place here? Very curious.*

Amanda watched as Sapphire flirted with the lady for a bit longer, then stood up and walked across the stage. She smiled at the adoring crowd as they set their bills down.

"Okay, pick up your five," she told Amanda.

Amanda did as she said, holding the bill in the air.

"Put it in my garter," she said.

Amanda paused.

"Go ahead," Sapphire urged. "Just slid it on up there. You know you want to."

Amanda giggled. "I feel silly."

Sapphire looked at her seriously. "You won't feel silly when you're walking off stage with a couple of hundred bucks."

Amanda nodded and slid the bill inside. As she did, Sapphire leaned down and pressed her breasts against her face. Amanda felt her hard nipples brush against her cheek.

"This is a common move," Sapphire said. "Learn it well. You'll probably going to be doing this a lot." She sat on the edge of the stage and draped her legs across Amanda's shoulders. "You're so fucking cute, Amanda. The ladies are going to be crawling all over you, you wait."

She lifted her skirt, giving Amanda a quick flash of her pink slit. She lowered her voice. "So, you see that woman on the other side?"

"Sitting by herself? Yeah, what's her story?"

"That's Lily, one of my regulars. She's been coming here every Friday for the last month, and every time she gets a private dance. She's a sweet girl, just a little awkward."

"Yeah, I can tell."

"Well, I'm going to see if you can join us tonight."

"Really?"

"We can have a lot of fun, the three of us. And it'll be a learning experience for you. I can show you some more moves.

Who knows, maybe you'll show me a few of your own. I know you've got them."

The music changed, and Sapphire stood up. "Come over and talk to her with me. I think together we can convince her."

Amanda left her empty drink and followed Sapphire. Lily clutched her drink and looked around nervously as they walked toward her.

"Lily, there's someone I'd like you to meet. This is Amanda. It's her first night."

"Hi, Amanda," Lily said. She smiled, then turned back to Sapphire. "Do you have time for a private dance later? You aren't busy tonight, are you?"

"Never too busy for you, dear," Sapphire said. "I've been looking forward to it all week." She leaned in and put her hand on Lily's shoulder. "How would you feel if Amanda joined us tonight? Would that be okay?"

Lily frowned. "I don't know. It's always just the two of us."

"I know." Sapphire reached across and slid her hand behind Amanda's shoulders. "But I think you'll like this. Amanda might really surprise you."

"Really?" Lily scrunched her nose as she considered.

She leaned in and whispered in Lily's ear. "And it will be twice the fun."

"Well, okay."

"Are you ready, Lily? We can start the dance now if you'd like."

Lily's eyes lit up. "Really? I usually have to wait for you."

"Not tonight." Sapphire took Lily's hand and led her down the hall, Amanda following a few steps behind. When Sapphire swiped her pass card, Amanda recognized the Water Room, the site of their first experience together.

"Glad to be back, Amanda?" Sapphire asked as they walked in.

Amanda smiled enthusiastically. She admired the room under its soft blue lighting, and noticed for the first time the subtle, aquatic shapes painted on the walls - mermaids, dolphins, and seashells. "I love it in here. It just feels so good."

"I know what you mean," Sapphire said. "I've spent some fantastic evenings in this room."

"I'll bet."

Lily set her purse on the table and sat on the couch, arms crossed. She looked from Sapphire to Amanda, then back again.

"Amanda's just going to watch at first," Sapphire assured Lily. "I want her to get the feeling of how a dance should be. Is that all right with you?"

"Sure. That's okay."

*Maybe she's warming up to me, but it's hard to tell by her body language. This lady really needs to loosen up.*

Amanda smiled to herself.

*And I think I can help her.*

The music faded, and a new song came on overhead. Sapphire moved in front of Lily and shook her hips to the beat. Amanda watched as Lily slid lower on the couch, inviting Sapphire to straddle her.

"How do you want to start tonight?" Sapphire asked. She moved her body closer to Lily's. "Slow and gentle?" She rocked softly, then slowly sped up. "Or hard and fast?"

"Gentle, please."

Sapphire eased up, smiling and gazing down at Lily. "Gentle it is. I know how you like it." She summoned Amanda over with a flick of her wrist, then undid the top two buttons on her shirt. As Amanda walked over, Sapphire pressed Lily's face between her breasts.

Lily sighed with pleasure and turned her head. She rubbed her cheek on Sapphire's chest and Amanda saw the look of bliss on her face.

*She's in heaven. I think the poor girl's in love with her.*

Lily sighed again, then looked up. "You're so beautiful," she murmured.

Sapphire gently unwrapped Lily's arms from her hips and gave a slow shake. "That's so sweet, Lily." She slid away and stood up. "You're my favorite. Do you know that?"

"You're my favorite, too." Lily frowned. "Is the song over already? I thought we had a few more minutes."

"No, I want to show Amanda a few of my moves. She's ready to learn, and this feels like a great time. How do you feel about that?"

Amanda stood by awkwardly as Lily eyed her.

"Okay," Lily said. She crossed her arms again and waited.

"Go ahead, Amanda," Sapphire urged. "Feel the music."

Amanda nodded and stepped forward.

*Well, here goes nothing.*

"Get into it. Feel it in your heart and hips." Sapphire smiled. "You can't go wrong if you trust yourself."

Amanda took another step forward, and Sapphire laughed.

"Here, let me help you." She walked around Amanda and put a hand on her hip, guiding her toward Lily. "Step in, get closer. Right up to her. Remember, the patron should be your only focus when you're giving a lap dance." She gave Amanda gentle push. "Go ahead. Lily's a lot of fun."

"I am?" Lily looked unsure. She uncrossed her arms and let them fall to her sides. Amanda noticed that she rubbed her fingers together anxiously.

*That must be a nervous habit. This girl's really wound up tight.*

"Of course you are," Sapphire said. "We always have a good time together, don't we?"

"Yes." Lily smiled and uncrossed her arms.

"Amanda can show you a good time, too." Sapphire pushed Amanda forward. She curved her palm and cupped Amanda's breast, grazing her nipple.

Amanda smiled to herself as her nipple hardened. She undid one of her shirt buttons and stepped forward, listening to the music and swaying to the rhythm. Lily sat still and expectant, as if waiting to be served.

"There you go, Amanda. Do you feel it now?"

Amanda teased her nipples between her fingers and moved even closer. She pressed her body against Lily's. Lily sighed and burrowed her face between Amanda's breasts. Amanda slid down and grabbed Lily gently by the hips, easing herself on to her lap.

"Wonderful, Amanda," Sapphire cried out. "You're doing great."

Amanda swayed back and forth on Lily's lap, grinding in time with the music. Lily's breathing became rapid as they moved in unison, and they looked into each other's eyes. Lily smiled.

*Okay, so this is promising.*

Amanda took her shirt the rest of the way off and placed it on the arm of the couch. She swayed back and forth on Lily's lap, twisting her nipples between her fingers. A warm buzz grew in her core, and she slid down deeper.

Amanda grabbed Lily's hand. "You can touch me if you want." Lily traced a nipple with her index finger, then brought her hand back shyly.

Amanda laughed and shook her head. She licked her palm, then slid it slowly across her breasts. Her nipples sent jolts of pleasure racing through her, and she sighed with pleasure. "Just like that, Lily. Don't be shy."

Lily smiled as she licked her fingers and rubbed Amanda's nipples.

Amanda arched her back, giving Lily a full view of her breasts. She pushed down hard as the throbbing increased in intensity.

*Wow, this is a real turn-on! I know I'm supposed to be getting her off, but damn.*

The song ended, and a new one started. Amanda reluctantly peeled away from Lily. She was aroused and energized now and wanted to keep going. She looked over at Sapphire, who stood a few feet away.

"How'd I do?" Amanda asked.

Sapphire walked over and patted Lily on the shoulder. "What do you think? How did she do?"

"She's good," Lily said. "I like how she feels."

"I'm so happy," Sapphire said. "I think Amanda's going to fit in great here." She rubbed Lily's arm. "You don't mind if she joins us for the next song? There are a few more things I want to show her."

Lily smiled. "Sure, that sounds like fun."

As the music started up again, Sapphire faced Lily and slowly plucked her nipples. She slid on to Lily's lap and thrust her chest in her face. Curling a finger, she invited Amanda to join them.

Sapphire slid her hands up Lily's thighs. "I want to show Amanda how we play together. Okay?"

Lily nodded. "Yes."

Sapphire pressed down with three fingers as Lily shook with excitement. She gave a loud moan and Sapphire stroked harder, using her other hand to guide Lily's hip.

"Trust your intuition," Sapphire told Amanda. "You'll get a feel for it after a while, figuring out what the patron needs in the moment." She continued to rub. "Do you know what Lily needs right now?"

"I have an idea," Amanda said.

"Now, Lily. Amanda's going to help me. You're sure you don't mind?"

"I don't mind. Just please don't stop. It feels so good."

"Dear Lily, we're just getting started." Sapphire moved Amanda closer with her arm. "Let us show you." She guided Amanda's hand and they stroked Lily together. Lily's panties were soaked through now. Sapphire placed her hand on the small of Amanda's back and pushed her forward gently.

Amanda's nipples were at mouth level, and Lily looked up, as if to ask permission. Amanda nodded as Lily hesitantly slid her tongue across one of her nipples. She took the other one between her fingers and pinched. Pleasure flowed through and she moaned.

"Slow down, girl," Sapphire whispered in her ear. "Make sure she gets her money's worth. Draw it out, make it last."

Amanda's pussy was wet now, and she didn't want to stop, but she obeyed. She slowed down and listened as Lily trembled beneath her.

"Watch me." Sapphire cradled Lily's pussy with her palm. Lily buckled and pushed upward, straining for her touch.

"No, don't stop," Lily murmured. "Please."

"Are you close, baby?" Sapphire glided her fingers down Lily's thighs.

"So close."

Sapphire winked at Amanda as she rubbed again. Lily shook and squirmed, frantically straining to come.

"Oh," Lily moaned. "Yes."

"Now," Sapphire commanded. She increased speed and Lily pressed her face into Amanda's chest, her groans muffled.

"Fuck," Lily cried. "Oh, fuck."

"There you go, baby," Sapphire said. "Let it out. Let it all out."

Lily shook with bliss as she came, then gave a little yelp and collapsed on the couch. Sapphire motioned for Amanda to stand up.

"Do you need to take a moment for yourself, Lily?"

Lily opened her eyes and nodded yes.

"Take a minute to recover, dear. It's fine."

Lily straightened up to a sitting position and reached for her purse. "I feel wonderful. How many songs was that?"

Sapphire smiled. "Lily, you didn't think we'd charge for a training session, did you?"

"Seriously?"

Amanda couldn't tell if the wetness around Lily's eyes was an aftereffect of her orgasm or something else.

*She's such a sensitive soul.*

"You did us a huge favor by letting Amanda join us," Sapphire said. "Her training is coming along great now, and it's all because of you. Thank you, Lily."

Lily beamed, then stood up and rushed into Sapphire's arms. "You're the best."

"No, you are. Stay here a while and compose yourself." Sapphire gave Amanda a gentle nudge on the arm. "Come on, girl, grab your stuff. We're going on stage."

Amanda followed Sapphire out of the Water Room and back to the main bar. She was buzzing with excitement. Helping Lily get off had been an unexpected pleasure, and she knew the night wasn't over yet. Not even close.

*I can't wait to see what happens next. I'm like it on this side of the stage.*

"Okay, we're up next," Sapphire said. She power-walked through the bar and Amanda had trouble keeping up. "Get up there and I'll show you some moves. Are you ready to go down the pole?"

"I don't know about that. I think I'll probably fall on my ass."

Sapphire laughed as she threw her purse on the stage and stepped up. "Don't worry about it. It takes a while to get used to it, but there's nothing to it. If you fall, you fall. I had a hell of a time when I first started. Bruises all over my ass. You'll toughen up."

"You make it seem so easy."

Sapphire held her hand out and pulled Amanda onto the stage. The group of five or six women circled around the stage applauded.

"So will you. You'll be a pro before you know it. Just give it some time." The bumper music ended, and a new song began. Amanda felt the slow, sensual song in her hips.

Sapphire made her rounds, chatting with a few of the patrons, giving them flashes of her breasts and collecting the bills they placed on the stage. She turned to Amanda, who stood by the pole.

"Go on, get up there." Sapphire pointed to the top of the pole. She blew a kiss to the crowd and walked over, then took Amanda's hands and placed them around the pole. Polished and faded from years of use, it was hard and sturdy. Amanda gripped it and waited for further instructions.

"Just play around. Feel it, get used to it," Sapphire said to her. "Start with a small loop. Twirl around with one hand and see how that feels."

"This is going to be so bad."

"It might. Do it anyway." Sapphire waved to the crowd. "They're a very forgiving audience. No one will notice if you mess up. If they do, they'll think it's cute. Just go for it."

"Okay, I'll give it a shot. But don't expect much." Amanda made a hesitant twirl as a loud roar of hooting and clapping arose from the crowd. She looked out and saw Ivy and Ophelia at the front of the stage, drinks in hand.

"Get it, girl," Ophelia shouted. "You've got this!"

Amanda blushed and made a stronger, faster attempt. The pole was firm in her hand, and she completed the loop easily. That gave her confidence, and she made another pass. She lifted herself up and swung around completely, kept her balance, and landed on her feet. Another round of applause from the audience.

"Yay, Amanda," Ivy called. "That was great!"

Sapphire took a turn on the pole, and Amanda watched as she crawled up to the top and slowly twirled down around one leg. Amanda admired her for a moment, then turned to the crowd. Ivy and Ophelia were waving, so she walked over to them.

"I told you I'd come by," Ivy said. She raised her glass and took a sip. "It's my first drink of the night. Cheers!"

"Have you learned any moves yet?" Ophelia asked.

Amanda shook her head. "Sadly, no."

"You will. You just have to figure out what they are. Think about what you like to see when you're on this side of the stage, then do that."

Amanda lifted her skirt up, revealing her thighs. "Like this?"

Ophelia smiled. "Come down here. I want to tell you something."

"Oh yeah? What's that?" She leaned in close, almost touching Ophelia.

"Watching you up there, I finally figured out your stage name. You're Phoenix."

Amanda smiled and slowly rubbed against her. "I'm Phoenix. I love it."

"I knew you would." Ophelia set a five in front of Ivy. "Now why don't you give some of that love to Ivy. She's been waiting for you to get up there all night."

Ivy swatted Ophelia's arm. "You stop that."

"You're telling me it wasn't your idea to sit here? Please." Ophelia looked up at Amanda and pointed to the bill. "She couldn't wait to get off work and come over here."

Amanda leaned down, getting closer to Ivy. "Is that true?"

"It's true," Ophelia said. "Come on, Phoenix, show us some moves. There's a ritual to it. Start with your top. Touch your curves, show them off. You've got to own it."

Amanda pressed her hands against her breasts, then plucked her nipples. "Like this?"

"Don't show me, show her." Ophelia waved the five in the air and set down again. "You're gonna earn this."

Amanda leaned in to Ivy, who smiled at her.

"You look wonderful up there," Ivy said. "Very sexy."

"Thanks." She leaned in further, pressing her breasts together in front of Ivy's face. She saw the look of desire in Ivy's eyes and smiled.

"Great job, Amanda," Ophelia said. "Seduce her with your eyes. Fuck her with your eyes. But don't give away too much at once. Make her want you."

Sapphire joined them and rubbed Amanda's shoulders. "How's it going over here?"

"Your girl's a little timid," Ophelia said. "You said she was wild."

"Give her some time," Sapphire said. She traced a line down Amanda's back and planted her hand on her ass. "She might have stage fright."

"Well, she needs to get over it."

Sapphire kissed Amanda on the cheek and whispered in her ear. "Remember our first night in the Water Room?"

Amanda smiled at the memory.

"Go over to Ivy. Show her what you can do."

Amanda walked toward the edge of the stage and drew closer, wrapping her arms around Ivy and nestling her face in her chest.

"You're lovely," Ivy purred.

"Thanks for humoring me. I like to pretend I know what I'm doing."

"Oh, you know what you're doing." Ivy looked at her seductively. "Don't play innocent with me."

Amanda took Ivy's hand and guided it up her thigh, just to the edge of her panties, then stopped.

The song ended, and Amanda started to stand up, but Ivy held her back. She had a mischievous look in her eye. "Hey, how about a dance?"

Sapphire came over and slid her pass key into Amanda's hand. "Go for it. It's the only way you're going to learn."

They bought a round of fresh drinks from Simone, then headed back.

"Do you have a favorite room?" Amanda asked. "There are so many I haven't explored yet."

"Okay, it's confession time. I've never even been back here before."

Amanda looked at her, confused. "You stop that. I figured you knew every inch of this place."

Ivy shook her head. "No. I don't usually go to the bar after work. But I wanted to tonight." She smiled. "I guess you could say I had a feeling."

The green light was on above the last door. Amanda swiped the pass card and led Ivy inside.

The room had recently been serviced. The leather couch smelled slightly of lemon, and the table for their drinks was spotless.

They set their drinks down. Ivy took a seat on the couch and motioned for Amanda to join her.

"Should we wait until the next song starts?" Amanda asked. She set her purse down and did a quick stretch. "I don't know how we're supposed to do this."

Ivy shook her head. "Amanda, I don't want to wait anymore. I'm so ready for this. I've wanted you for a long time."

"Is that right?" Amanda smiled as a warm buzz of anticipation returned.

"Oh, yes. Ever since the first night you showed up with Miss Trent. I could tell you were someone I wanted to know better."

"You're sweet."

"You think so?" Ivy rubbed her thighs seductively. "Why don't you come here and find out how sweet I am?"

Amanda took a few steps toward the couch and slid onto Ivy's lap. She took Ivy's hands in hers and led them to her ass. "It's okay to touch back here, you know."

Ivy smiled. "Yeah, I know. I've always been curious about what goes on in these rooms. I see the ladies walking out and they look so satisfied." She leaned in and whispered in Amanda's ear. "Come closer. I have something for you."

"Intriguing. I can't wait." As Ivy traced her fingers along Amanda's sides, a warm buzz welled up and burned inside her.

"You have magic hands," Amanda said. "I don't know what you have planned, but I like where you're going."

"I'm going to use my magic hands on you. Are you ready?"

Amanda held Ivy's hands as she ground down in her lap. "Hold up. I thought this was supposed to be about you. Aren't you the customer tonight?"

Ivy licked her lips. "But don't you see? This is what I want." She took her hands back and stroked Amanda's thighs, moving closer to her pussy with every pass.

Amanda squirmed and spread her legs wider. "You can do anything you want right now."

Ivy smiled. "Yeah?" She softly patted the front of Amanda's skirt, then slid her hand under and up.

A spark shot through Amanda, and she moaned. "Definitely."

"Could I do this?" Ivy leaned in and kissed Amanda's neck, then moved her head down and nuzzled against her breasts.

"Of course."

"What about this?" Ivy moved her hands around to the small of Amanda's back and let her fingers explore the waistband of her panties. Ivy's fingers were soft and warm, and she yearned for them. Amanda scooted up and they moved further down to her ass.

"Mm-hmm." Amanda slipped out of her top again and played with her nipples, squeezing them until they were hard again.

Ivy moved Amanda's hands away and took her breast in her mouth, rolling the nipple around with her tongue. She gently moved Amanda onto the couch and straddled her, moving her lips from breast to breast, then slid down until she was on the floor.

She tugged at Amanda's skirt. "This is coming off right now."

Amanda helped slide it off and it landed on the floor. Ivy opened Amanda's legs and kissed her inner thighs. Amanda spread her legs wide as her wetness merged with Ivy's open mouth. She sighed as Ivy moved her tongue up and twirled around her nub, a circular motion gradually increasing in intensity. She pushed down into the couch, her back arched, and twisted her nipples between her fingers.

Ivy pulled in closer, gripping Amanda's ass with both hands, and buried her face in her pussy. She licked her clit with reverence, pressing down hard until Amanda lost control and cried out. Ivy slowed down, then slid upward and embraced her.

"Wow. You have a magic tongue, too," Amanda said.

"Maybe it's just a magic room."

Amanda looked around at the blue walls and smiled. "Maybe it is."

"It feels like we're under the sea, don't you think?" Ivy leaned over and took a sip of her drink.

"It's really cool," Amanda agreed. "Some night we should explore the other rooms. There are three more on this floor, and more upstairs. I want to experience them all."

"I like the way you think. I'm into this plan."

Amanda took a drink. "Hey, aren't I supposed to be giving you a lap dance or something?"

"Yeah. I guess we got kind of sidetracked."

"I guess we did." Amanda set her drink down and stood up. "Well, there's still time to get back on track. If you want."

"I'm glad I could be part of your learning experience." Ivy leaned back on the couch and spread her legs. "I'm up for anything."

"Is that right?" Amanda straddled Ivy, grabbing her thighs. She sank into Ivy's lap, and they rocked back and forth for a moment.

"Your first night as a dancer should be special, don't you think?" Ivy asked.

"It already is." Amanda leaned in and slid her breasts in Ivy's face, grinding down as her cunt throbbed. She held Ivy's head with one hand and looked into her eyes. Ivy nodded yes, and Amanda kissed her, slowly and deeply, while she slid her other hand down. Ivy moaned with pleasure.

Amanda rubbed the outside of Ivy's skirt with two fingers, pressing down hard.

"Right there," Ivy cried out. "That's the spot."

Amanda smiled as she continued to rub. "Not quite. Your skirt is in the way."

"Well, let's do something about that."

Once her skirt was off, Amanda licked her fingers and dove under Ivy's panties. She gently spread Ivy's pussy as she kissed her. Her middle finger glided above Ivy's clit, and she stroked it back and forth softly.

"Oh, fuck," Ivy moaned. "Faster. Please."

Amanda smiled at Ivy's pink, clean-shaven pussy. She moved her fingers inside and rubbed Ivy's clit.

"That feels so good," Ivy said. "You're amazing."

"You're not the only one with magic hands." Amanda kept rubbing and kissed her again.

Ivy closed her eyes and sighed with pleasure. Amanda felt Ivy tense up as she came. She pulled her in and held her as she quaked with pleasure. "There it is. That's what I wanted."

Ivy slowly opened her eyes and smiled. "Damn, girl. Where did you learn that?"

"Wouldn't you like to know?" She hesitated a moment, then smiled. "Maybe one day I'll tell you."

"You'd better." She leaned back on the couch, her face glowing. "You know, I think you have a long career ahead of you."

When they got back to the Lounge, the stage shows had ended, and the bar had cleared out. Only a few tables remained. Sapphire and Ophelia sat at the bar drinking cocktails and chatting with Simone.

Sapphire smiled as Amanda and Ivy walked up together. "Well, well, well. How was that for your first night, Amanda?"

"She needs to work here all the time," Ivy said.

Sapphire took a sip of her drink. "You're right about that." She turned to Amanda. "You fit right in here. How about it, girl? When are you coming over to the dark side?"

"I mean, the book is nearly done. Vivian's going to New York to meet with the publisher next week, and I'm not sure what's happening after that. Erica hasn't said anything about new projects."

"I know Vivian likes you, you'd just have to ask her and you're in."

"I might just do that. I wouldn't mind coming down here and playing with you all."

Sapphire winked at her. "And if not, Sam's Clubhouse is always hiring."

"Ha. Don't even joke about that."

Ivy stroked Amanda's back. "Come to the Obsidian," she said. "You know you want to."

"Besides, I still need to teach you some of my private dance techniques," Ophelia said.

"They're incredible." Sapphire smiled and touched her arm. "Ophelia can do amazing things."

"I believe it," Amanda said.

"Find me the next time you're here," Ophelia said. "I'll show you what I mean."

Amanda took a sip of her drink, perfectly made by Simone. She looked at the three beautiful women sitting around her and smiled.

*Why do I get the feeling the fun's just getting started around here?*

Amanda clicked send on the email and slowly exhaled. She finally finished her last task of the day, which was also the last task of the Obsidian Lounge project. She stood up and felt her knee crack, then rubbed it and frowned.

*I don't like that. Waitressing might have sucked, but at least I was active. Sitting at a desk all day isn't good for me.*

She walked downstairs to the kitchen and poured a glass of wine. Time to celebrate. As she took her first sip, she saw Erica in the doorway, her sensual legs clad in a pair of black slacks.

"I just sent the last of the transcripts," she said.

"Got 'em," Erica replied as she walked past. "I just need to make a few revisions and I'll send them off to Vivian."

"I can't believe that was the last interview. Is it really done?"

"That was it. After Vivian sends it to her publisher, the manuscript is complete. Mind if I join you?"

"I'd love some company after being stuck up in that office all day. Can I offer you a glass?"

"Of my own wine? Why, thank you, Amanda." Erica laughed. "I'm teasing. We both deserve a drink for getting through that one. It was the most complicated project I've ever done."

"Yeah. Me, too."

"Well, you did great. Transcribing all those hours of interviews couldn't have been easy."

"It wasn't," Amanda agreed. "So, what's next for you? What literary adventures await Miss Erica Trent?"

"Hard to say. I don't have anything lined up at the moment. A friend has invited me to Paris for the weekend, and I may take her up on the offer. It's been far too long since I've visited Europe."

"Wow, Paris. That's exciting."

"Have you ever been?"

"Come on, Erica." Amanda held her glass of wine awkwardly. "You know I've never even left the States."

"Oh, that's right. Silly me. Well, I recommend it highly. Travel has enriched my life in so many ways."

Amanda took a sip. "I can only imagine."

"Well, someday you won't have to imagine. Maybe sooner than you think."

"Maybe. Until then, I need to check with Diane and make sure I can still move back in."

"Of course you can, Amanda. I'm sure Diane is eagerly awaiting your return." Erica paced the kitchen floor. "In the meantime, have you thought about what you'd like to do for work?"

"I really haven't," she admitted. "I've been able to save a bit, so I have a cushion for the first time in my life. So that's nice." She frowned. "But I know I can't live on that forever. I'm sure I'll figure something out."

"You said you enjoyed the night you worked at the Obsidian Lounge."

Amanda thought back to her evening with Clara, Julie, and Miss Spencer.

*I got to play with three beautiful women, came hard, and walked away with a bunch of money in my purse. Yeah, I'll say I enjoyed that.*

"Oh, I did. Very much."

"Well, all you'd have to do is call. I've spoken with Vivian, and she told me she'd love to have you."

"She did? Cool. Yes, I'll call when I get back to town."

"That's great, Amanda. I know you'll enjoy your time there."

*I already have.*

Late that evening, there was a soft knock on her door. Amanda looked up and set her book on the nightstand.

"Come on in," she called.

Erica stuck her head inside. "Amanda, I hate to talk business again, but something's come up."

Amanda sat up. "What is it?"

"I just got off the phone with Vivian. She's meeting with her publisher in two days. She asked for you."

"Why me?"

"She'd like you to fly to New York and meet her. She was quite insistent and said that your flight and hotel will be paid for." Erica pulled out her phone and tapped on it. "I'll send you her private number. Please call as soon as you can. It sounds important."

Once Erica left, Amanda dialed the number and Vivian answered immediately.

"Amanda, thank you for calling back."

"Of course."

"So, you'll come?"

"I'd love to."

"Wonderful. Clara and I got here yesterday."

Amanda smiled.

*Clara's with her? Interesting...*

"I have an important meeting with the publisher. They have a few questions about the manuscript and asked if you could be there."

"Me? Why? Is anything wrong?"

"I'm sure it's nothing. Just some last-minute questions. I'll email with your flight information tonight. I've asked Erica to have her driver take you to the airport. There will be a taxi waiting when you land. I'll see you tomorrow, Amanda. And thank you."

Amanda hung up.

*What do they want to talk to me about?*

Clara was waiting in the lobby. She was dressed comfortably in jeans and a black wool sweater and looked as gorgeous as ever. Amanda gave her a long hug, gripping her tight and letting their bodies linger together a bit longer than she intended.

Clara responded by giving her a peck on the cheek. "Welcome to the Big Apple, darling."

"So exciting, right?"

"You've really never been before?"

"I've barely left Oregon. But it's been on my list for years. I want to see the Statue of Liberty and Times Square. I want to see it all."

"Well, we won't be doing much sightseeing on this trip, unfortunately. So far, all I've done is try to calm Vivian down. She's really nervous about this meeting."

"I'll help any way I can. Do you have anything special in mind?"

Clara smiled. "I'm glad you asked. The plan is to take her out tonight. She needs to get her mind off it for a while. I have a place in mind, and I think you're going to love it."

"Sounds good to me. I'm always up for a new adventure."

"I knew you'd be on board."

"Ha, like there was any doubt."

"Okay, let's get you set up in your room. Vivian has a suite booked for herself, and our rooms are just down the hall."

"Mmm. That's convenient."

Clara smiled and rubbed Amanda's shoulder. "It will be."

Her room was even more luxurious than the one she'd shared with Erica in Vancouver. The bed was a King, and the television took up half the wall. A small glass bowl filled with expensive chocolates sat in the middle of the coffee table. Amanda sat her roller bag on the floor and opened the curtains.

*Wow. What a view of the city. I'd love to take a day and just wander around sometime.*

She spent a few moments staring out the window, enchanted by the skyline. Then she unpacked a bit and rested for a few minutes.

There was a knock on the door.

"Come in," she said.

Vivian walked in, dressed in a t-shirt, jeans, and sneakers. She seemed preoccupied. "Clara told me you arrived. I just wanted to check in and see that you made it here safely."

"Everything's great so far, thank you."

"Thanks for coming on such short notice."

"Of course."

*I see what Clara means. She's wound up so tight.*

"I appreciate it. You'll join us for dinner this evening, won't you?"

"Of course. When should I be ready?"

"Our reservations are at seven." She pointed to her clothes. "I need to get changed first. Come over in a bit and we can have a cocktail before we go out."

"That sounds great."

"Fantastic. I'll see you soon." She looked at Amanda. "And thanks again. Having you here means a lot to me."

Amanda showered and dressed in one of her best work outfits.

*I know Vivian's seen me in this before, but I only have so many outfits. It's time to go shopping again. I can't keep wearing the same three things over and over.*

She knocked on Vivian's door at six-thirty. Vivian answered, wearing a fancy black dress and a red sweater.

"Come in, Amanda," she said. "We were going over our plans for the evening."

Clara waved from one of the beds. "Grab a drink, girl. "

"What can I offer you?" Vivian asked. "I'm afraid the minibar only has one kind of wine."

"I'm not picky," Amanda said. "Whatever you're having is fine."

"Clara, would you be a dear and fetch Amanda a bottle?"

"My pleasure." Clara walked over to the bar and returned with a small bottle and a plastic cup.

"My usual accommodations weren't available," Vivian explained. "Ordinarily, my suite would be more upscale, and the bar would be fully stocked. But this hotel is close to the publisher's office, and that was more important for this trip."

"What's important is for you to have a good time tonight," Clara said. "Amanda and I will see to that." She winked at Amanda. "I have it all planned. We're going out tonight."

"Oh, are we?" Vivian looked from Clara to Amanda, then back again.

"We are," Clara said, "and I'll have no arguments from you, Miss Starr."

Vivian chuckled. "I wouldn't dream of it."

Dinner was lovely, and afterward they took a cab to the Peacock Room. Clara sat in the middle, and Amanda looked out the window.

"This was my favorite club when I was younger," Vivian said. "Some people consider it the second-best lesbian club in the United States."

"After the Obsidian," Clara said. "Of course."

"Of course." Vivian beamed with pride.

"I've only been here once before," Clara said. She reached down and softly touched Amanda's thigh.

"That was a wonderful evening," Vivian said. "I'll never forget it."

"And we'll have another one tonight." Clara turned to Amanda. "This place is nothing like the Obsidian. It's not on the same scale." She smiled. "But I think you're going to love it."

She squeezed Amanda's thigh again, harder this time, and a gentle throb of passion rose as Amanda looked out the window at the tall buildings and traffic.

*I love it already.*

It really was nothing like the Obsidian. It was smaller, a single level with only one stage. And old. Amanda could almost feel its history as they walked in.

*So, this is the East Coast. I think I like it.*

It was clean, though, and had a classy feel - the same sassy, feminine energy she loved about the Obsidian. Clara ordered a round of drinks and they sat at a small table in the corner, where Amanda had a view of the entire club.

"I didn't tell Mary I was coming," Vivian said. "She's probably not here, anyway."

"Mary is the owner," Clara explained. "They've been friends for years."

"She helped me start the Obsidian before she moved here," Vivian said. "Along with Jessica Frost, we ran that place the first few years. Those were good times."

Clara nodded toward the stage. A tall blonde woman wearing a red and black outfit entertained the crowd. "Do you recognize her, Vivian? I remember her from last time we were here."

Vivian smiled. "I certainly do." She patted Clara on the shoulder. "Thanks for this. You were right, it's just what I needed. I'm so nervous now that the book is finally coming out, and I've been letting it get to me."

"I know," Clara said. "That's why we're going to let off a little steam tonight. You deserve it." She smiled and raised her glass. The ladies toasted, then sipped their drinks.

Vivian stood up. "Let's go down and sit at the stage before her set is over. She might not remember us, but I certainly remember her."

Amanda followed them across the room, and they sat down at the rack. The dancer saw them and walked over, her large breasts on display.

"Nice choice," Amanda whispered to Clara.

"You just wait," Clara said, and squeezed her thigh again. Amanda felt the familiar warm flow rise and smiled to herself.

*I guess I'll have to. Patience. I'll get her alone soon.*

The dancer walked up to Vivian and laid her body across the stage. She looked up with deep blue eyes and rubbed her breasts. "Welcome back, Miss Starr. It's so nice to see you again. It's been a while."

"See? She does remember you," Clara said.

"Of course I do." The dancer leaned in and slid down to the stage floor, then pressed her breasts against Vivian's chest. "I'll never forget that night. So, what brings you to town this time?"

"We're having a girls' night out," Clara said. "And we brought a friend with us. This is Amanda."

"Lovely to meet you, Amanda. I'm Belle." She turned back to Vivian. "You certainly know how to choose your companions, Miss Starr. So, are you all looking for a little fun tonight? What's on your agenda?"

"We're going to see where the night takes us," Vivian said. "Isn't that right, Clara?"

"That's right. We're celebrating tonight," Clara said.

"You're in the right place, ladies," Belle said. "I love helping people celebrate. It's what I do best."

Vivian excused herself to the restroom. When she was gone, Clara curled a finger at Belle seductively.

"We want you to show Miss Starr a good time tonight. She's been under a lot of stress lately." Amanda watched Clara slip her a couple of bills. "Will that cover it?"

Belle smiled as she slid the money into her garter. "Honey, I'd dance for Vivian Starr for free. That lady is a legend around here. But, yes, this will cover it nicely. I'll pull out all the stops." She turned to Amanda. "Maybe later I'll get to spend a little time with you. I can tell you're a lot of fun."

"Amanda is also a dancer," Clara said.

"That doesn't surprise me at all." Belle leaned in and brushed her cheek across Amanda's. "She has such a sensual vibe."

"I only danced for the first time the other night," Amanda protested.

"I'll bet you were amazing." Belle turned to Clara. "Well, was she?"

"I wouldn't know. I wasn't there." Clara slid her hand down Amanda's thigh again. "Maybe next time."

"How did it feel, Amanda?" Belle asked. "Did you enjoy it? I just love dancing. It makes me feel alive."

"I was a little nervous at first," Amanda admitted. "But I got into it after a while. I had a couple of incredible teachers."

"Do you mean Sapphire and Ophelia?" Clara asked.

Amanda nodded. "Oh, yeah."

"Wow, now I'm jealous."

Vivian sat back down. "How's everyone doing? Do you need anything?"

"We're fine," Clara said. "But we have something for you."

Belle picked up her clothes as the next dancer approached the stage. She leaned in to Vivian.

"Come with me, dear. I have my instructions." She winked. "And I know just how I'm going to carry them out. It's your lucky night, Miss Starr."

Vivian smiled. "Oh, Clara. You're so thoughtful. Thank you."

Clara waved goodbye, then turned to Amanda. "She really needed this. Maybe she'll calm down for a while. I had to do something."

"I think it's perfect. Now we can spend some time together alone."

"Not yet," Clara said. "I have another plan."

The next dancer climbed up the pole and twirled down on one leg. She wore a black leather cap and black lace leggings. Her long, brunette hair covered her large breasts. Clara and Amanda set their bills on the stage as she made the rounds, finally approaching them.

"Hi, ladies. I'm Lacy. Where are you visiting from?"

"What makes you think we're tourists?" Clara asked.

"Are you saying you're not?" Lacy pinched her nipples provocatively as she lay on the stage in front of them. "Come on. I have an eye for these things."

Clara laughed. "Guilty. Come a little closer and I'll tell you where we're from."

Lacy leaned in and Clara whispered in her ear. She nodded and smiled, then turned to Amanda.

"You have a good friend there, Amanda. She just told me I'm supposed to rock your world."

"Oh, she did, did she?"

Lacy brushed her bare breasts against Amanda. "She did." She sat on the edge of the stage and wrapped her legs around Amanda's neck, pressing herself close. Her thighs were tan and muscular, and she smelled faintly like rose. Amanda let herself be enveloped, savoring every moment.

"How do you like the city so far?" Lacy asked. "Have you been to any of the fancy tourist sights yet?"

"Not really. Just the airport and the hotel."

"And now you've been to the Peacock Room."

Amanda nodded. "Yes."

Lacy traced her nipples with her fingers. "You picked a great night. I'm feeling frisky." Lacy kissed her on the cheek, then stood up and walked to the other end of the stage, putting on a show for the crowd.

"What did you tell her?" Amanda said.

"Just a little white lie. I told her this was your first time at a club, and to make the private dance she's giving you extra special."

Amanda grinned. "You're so bad."

"It's just a little harmless fun."

"You know she's going to figure out you lied."

"Probably. But we might as well have some entertainment tonight. Who knows how long Vivian will be? That woman has stamina."

"Oh, does she?"

Amanda tried to imagine how Vivian made love. It wasn't hard to do, and she spent a few moments swept away in fantasy.

When the song ended, Lacy walked over and offered her arm to Amanda. "Shall we?"

"Do you mind if I come along?" Clara asked.

"The more the merrier." Lacy smiled. "You're such a supportive friend."

Amanda and Clara gathered their coats and purses and followed her to the back. The room wasn't as large or fancy as those at the Obsidian, but it had an air of class. Different, yet familiar.

"Have a seat, ladies," Lacy said. "I'll take care of everything."

Amanda and Clara set their drinks down and sat next to each other on the couch. As Lacy approached, Clara pointed at Amanda. Lacy nodded and smiled in delight as she moved in rhythm with the overhead music.

"Things are a little different here than you're probably used to," Lacy said. "Unfortunately, there's no touching allowed between dancer and customer."

"Oh, that's right," Clara said. "I totally forgot about that stupid law."

"It is a stupid law," Lacy said. "Lucky for us, there are a couple of ways around it."

"What about me?" Clara asked. "I'm not a dancer or a customer. Who am I allowed to touch?"

Lacy winked at her. "You can enjoy the show however you want, love."

Clara stroked the outside of her skirt. "Oh, I intend to. Don't mind me."

Lacy turned her attention back to Amanda. "Where was I?" She gently plucked her hard nipples, teasing them between her fingers. "Now, there's no law that says I can't touch myself."

She leaned in. "And the same goes for you. You can explore yourself all you want, Amanda."

Clara rubbed Amanda's thigh with her other hand. "And there's nothing that says I can't touch her, right?"

Lacy nodded as she gently bit her bottom lip. "You catch on quick, Clara." She teased her breasts an inch from Amanda's face. "It's a good thing you're here, or I'd be in violation of the law for sure."

"Is that right?" Amanda asked. She sighed as Clara's fingers moved up her thighs and made their way to her lap.

*Finally. I've been waiting for this all night.*

Clara stroked her with two fingers, and Amanda adjusted herself on the couch, spreading her legs wide.

"Are you sure you've never been to a club before?" Lacy asked with a smile. "You seem to know your way around here pretty good." She turned to Clara. "Well?"

Clara laughed and continued to stroke. "Guilty. Amanda actually helped write the book of the Obsidian Lounge."

Lacy's eyes lit up. "Really? I'd heard rumors. When is it coming out?"

"Next week, I think."

"Cool. I know there are going to be a lot of hot stories in there."

Amanda smiled. "Yes, a few made it in." She sighed as Clara found her clit. "But you should have heard some of the ones that didn't."

Amanda reached up and felt her breasts through her shirt, teasing her hard nipples. Lacy's breasts were a few inches from her face, and she resisted the urge to lick them.

*Rules are rules. I guess. But, damn.*

"So, you've really seen the book?" Lacy asked. She stepped back and removed her skirt and black lace panties. Her pussy was shaved clean, and she licked her fingers before rubbing herself. "I hope it's worth the wait."

"It was a lot of work," Amanda said began, but stopped talking as a moan escaped her lips. "Oh, Clara, my God."

"What?" Clara asked innocently.

"How do you do it?" Amanda felt her orgasm rise as Clara fingered her wet pussy. "So good."

"The same way you do. I feel."

Lacy stepped forward and placed her pussy so close to Amanda's face it was almost touching. Her lips were spread a bit, and Amanda saw her pink clit peeking out.

"Remember, no touching," Lacy said.

"Damn this backward state."

"I know, right?" Lacy rubbed herself, and Amanda felt the wetness against her face. "Bunch of Puritans on the East Coast."

When Lacy and Amanda finally came, it was at the same time.

*Yes, so far New York City is alright with me. I'm coming back here again when I can spend more time.*

Back at the bar, Amanda and Clara got another round of drinks. They took seats at the stage and watched the dancer. Amanda studied her, how she worked the pole, how she greeted and flirted with the patrons.

"You like her," Clara said. "Don't you?"

"She's great. She's such a natural." Amanda took a sip of her drink. "I felt like such a goofball on stage the other night."

"You can't compare yourself to other dancers. You'll find your own style." She smiled. "I'm sure of it."

"You're sweet," Amanda said. "We'll see. They said they want me to come back next week."

Clara touched her leg again, and Amanda shivered with pleasure. She was still wet from her orgasm, her thighs slick with juice.

Vivian walked up with Belle. "I hope you haven't been waiting too long." She squeezed Belle's hand. "We lost track of time back there."

"We didn't mind waiting," Clara said. "Did we, Amanda?"

"Not at all. There's so much to do here."

"I'm glad," Vivian said. She was flushed and beaming, more relaxed than Amanda had seen her in weeks.

"I'm on stage next," Belle said. "Thank you for a lovely time, Miss Starr."

"The pleasure was mine," Vivian said, and giggled. She watched Belle as she walked away, then turned back. "Clara, be a dear and call a cab for us. I'd like to go back to the hotel now."

"Of course." Clara pulled out her phone and dialed.

"Perhaps we'll have a nightcap at the hotel." Vivian sat down next to them. "I barely touched my drink all night."

Back in Vivian's suite, Clara poured three glasses of wine. Amanda sat on one of the beds, Vivian on the other.

"That was such a great idea, Clara," Vivian said, accepting a glass. "Thank you for thinking of me."

"What would you do without me?"

"I hope I never find out." She leaned back on the bed, her skirt inching up her leg, and Amanda glimpsed her black panties. "Let's just get through this meeting tomorrow. After that, maybe I can relax."

"The book is a go, right?" Amanda asked.

"You've never had the pleasure of dealing with publishers before, have you?" Vivian took a sip of wine and set her glass on the nightstand.

Amanda shook her head. "No. Erica has told me a few stories, though."

"I'll bet she has." Vivian sighed. "Well, they always want changes. But what Mr. John Samson is going to discover tomorrow is that this is my story, and I'm telling it my way. If a couple of egos get hurt, or a few people aren't happy with some stories, they can deal with it. This is about integrity."

"Of course it is, Vivian."

"I have nothing to be ashamed of. Yes, there were some wild times in the old days. But I built my business on my own terms. I'll always be proud of that."

"I'm glad I could be a small part of it," Amanda said.

"Amanda, you've been a huge part of it. Erica told me how hard you worked and how much you contributed to the manuscript."

"That was nice of her."

"She meant it. You did a good job. We'll find out how good soon." Vivian yawned. "It's time for me to turn in. Tonight really took it out of me." She smiled. "In a good way."

"We should go," Clara said. "I'll walk you over to your room, Amanda."

"Yes, you girls get some rest. Don't stay up too late. We'll get up early and have a nice breakfast before the meeting."

As soon as they were in the hall, Clara pulled Amanda in and kissed her passionately. "Oh my God, I've wanted to do that all night."

"Me too."

Clara swiped her key card with one hand and pulled Amanda inside with the other. "I've missed you so much," she said as the door closed, then set her purse on the floor. She moved Amanda gently toward the wall, cupping her face with her hands, and gave her another sensual kiss.

"I've missed you too," Amanda said. "It's been too long since we were together."

"I'm glad it's not just me." She rubbed Amanda's arms, then patted her stomach.

Her fire was lit again, and Amanda pulled her in close. They kissed briefly, then Clara moved them over to the bed.

Clara straddled her, holding her legs apart, then leaned in. "I want you."

"Take me," Amanda said. "I'm all yours."

Clara smiled and slipped Amanda's shoes off, then her socks. She cupped Amanda's ass and kissed the inside of her thighs. "Take your shirt off," she said.

Amanda complied, unbuttoning her shirt and letting it fall to the floor.

"And your bra." Clara went straight for her breasts, licking one nipple, then the other. Amanda leaned back on the bed and smiled.

"Now that skirt. You know it's got to go."

Clara laid down next to Amanda and licked her fingers. She moved them down to Amanda's pussy and kissed her while she explored.

"I've missed this little lady," she said. She rubbed harder.

Amanda moaned as Clara intuitively found her clit. "You know just how to touch me."

"And I'm just getting started," Clara said. "Close your eyes and leave it all to me. I want to see you come again." She made quick figure-eights with her fingers, and Amanda sighed.

A few seconds later Amanda felt soft hands on her thighs as Clara shifted position and found her nub. Clara licked her gently, but her orgasm built quickly. She cried out as she came.

"Will you let me return the favor?" she asked, after she had caught her breath.

"Please," Clara said. "I'm ready for you." She stood up and walked over to her suitcase. "I just have one request."

"Sure, what is it?"

Clara reached in the bottom of her suitcase and brought out a small case. She opened it and held out a small black vibrator. "Use this on me?"

"Of course."

"It's the only way I'm able to come lately."

"The only way? Really?"

"I don't know what's wrong with me." Clara frowned. "It's probably stress." She sat back down on the bed. "This is the only thing that works."

"I don't think I'll need it, Clara. I have a few other ways. Don't you remember our night on the coast?"

"Of course I do. It was the last time anyone went down on me."

"You stop that."

"It's true. The only person I've been with since then is Vivian, and she doesn't really reciprocate like that."

"You and Vivian, huh? Well, I had my suspicions."

"We have a very one-sided relationship," Clara said. "I know I can't change her. I've tried for so long. Sometimes you just have to take what you can get."

"Really? But you deserve so much better than that."

Clara sighed. "Yeah, I know."

"Here, let me show you." Amanda took the vibrator from Clara and set it on the nightstand. "I'll use this on you, but only if you'll let me try something else first. Do we have a deal?"

Clara smiled. "Okay."

Amanda pushed Clara gently down on to the bed, then scooted down and nestled her face between her legs. She gazed at Clara's pussy and brought her lips close, nibbling softly.

Clara moaned and spread her legs wider. Amanda scooted back up and pressed her body against Clara's as she used two fingers on her. Her fingers slid across Clara's clit effortlessly. It felt so right.

"Oh, Amanda, it's been too long."

"Shh. Just enjoy it."

"You're so good to me. Fuck."

Amanda rubbed her clit in small circles. "Shut up and come for me," she said. She smiled as Clara spasmed, then held her gently and covered her face with kisses.

The phone rang at seven the next morning. It was Vivian.

"Good morning, Amanda. Breakfast will be in half an hour, then we're heading down to the publisher's office. I'll have Clara come get you."

"Okay, I'll be ready."

Amanda showered and put on her best business casual outfit, another one of her purchases from Ruth's store. Breakfast was in the restaurant downstairs, then they took a cab to the publisher's office.

The secretary welcomed them and announced their arrival. Mr. Sampson came out of his office a few moments later. A tall, clean-shaven man in his fifties, he had gray hair and glasses.

*He's just how I expected a New York publisher to look. What a cliché.*

"Welcome, ladies. Come into my office and we'll get started."

Once inside, they sat at a large conference table, Vivian and Mr. Sampson on opposite ends.

"Is everything set, John?" Vivian asked. "There aren't any issues I need to be aware of?"

"No issues, per se. Just some clarification, if you would." Mr. Sampson looked around the table. "Tell me, who conducted the interview with Jessica Frost?"

"The three of us and Erica Trent," Vivian said. "We were all in the room."

"I see. And do I understand correctly that no one recorded the interview?"

"That's right. Jessica refused, for some reason known only to her." Vivian shrugged. "She almost wasted an entire trip for us."

"So, one of you wrote it from memory, or what? How did that work?"

"Amanda?" Vivian looked at her expectantly. "Would you please answer the question?"

"Well, sure," Amanda said. "Erica and I wrote down as much as we could remember." She shrugged. "It was the best we could do under the circumstances."

"I understand," Mr. Sampson said. "I need to clarify that this company assumes no liability."

"Liability?" Vivian asked. "What possible liability could there be?"

"Any sort of legal action that could result from publication." He handed a piece of paper to Amanda. "Would you pass that to Vivian, please?"

"What is this?" Vivian asked.

"Strictly a formality. We have to cover our interests as well."

"I see. And this is all because of Jessica Frost?"

Mr. Sampson nodded. "Now, I'm sure nothing will come of it. If you will just sign, we can get on with our days. I'm sure you're as busy as I am."

"Fine. I think Jessica has forgotten that I was around then, too. And I have an excellent memory. I don't understand why she's so afraid of the truth." Vivian signed the paper and handed it back. "I stand by *The Secret History*, John. It's too bad you aren't willing to do the same."

"Hopefully we'll never need this." He handed the paper to Amanda. "I also need a witness to sign it. Otherwise, this could have all been done electronically."

Amanda looked at the document. It seemed straightforward enough. She signed it and passed it back.

"That's all I need." Mr. Sampson stood up. "Enjoy the rest of your trip, ladies. Do you have any other plans?"

"We're flying back tonight." Vivian stood up as well. "When is the book going to press?"

"I'll send the proofs off tonight. It will be at the printers early next week."

"Fantastic. Well, we'll be going now."

"Thanks again for your time, ladies. Please understand, it's just business."

Amanda picked Diane out of the crowd right away. Dressed in a small white t-shirt and skinny black jeans, a black beanie covering her short blonde hair, she looked like a typical Portlander.

"There's someone I want you two to meet," she told Clara and Vivian as they rolled their suitcases behind them and walked through security.

She gave Diane a warm hug. "These are my friends, Clara and Vivian."

"From the Obsidian Lounge, right?" Diane offered her hand to Vivian. "It's great to meet you both."

"You as well, dear."

Clara took her hand next. "I was hoping I'd meet you someday," she said.

"Would you like a ride home, Amanda?" Vivian asked. "My driver is waiting outside."

"Oh, no thanks. Diane is here."

"Yeah, I'm parked in the lot," Diane said.

"I see. Well, until next time." Vivian gave Amanda a hug. "Thanks again for your help. Having you around made everything so much better."

"Of course. I can't wait until the book comes out."

"You'll get one of the first copies. I'll even sign it for you." Vivian laughed. "Who knows? It might be worth something someday."

"When's your next shift at the Lounge?" Clara asked.

"I'm going to take a few days to get settled back in my apartment, but I'll be back Saturday night."

"Great. I'll see you then." Clara turned to Diane. "You should come, too. Let Amanda know, and I'll make sure you I get you on the list."

"That would be amazing," Diane said. "Thank you so much."

Amanda hugged Clara. "I'll see you soon."

They parted ways, Vivian and Clara taking the escalator down to baggage claim, while Diane and Amanda walked together out to the parking structure.

Her room was exactly how she'd left it, just a little stuffy from being unoccupied for three months. Amanda turned on a fan, opened the window, and let the room air out. She changed the sheets and bedding, then scrubbed the tub and took a long bath. Later, she had Chinese food delivered. Her bank account was larger than it had ever been, thanks to the money she'd put away working on *The Secret History*.

*At least I don't have to get another job right away. That's really sweet.*

She spent the rest of the night on the couch, watching old sitcoms and eating snacks. It was good to be back.

Lawrence came by the next day with the last of her clothes from Trent Manor. Amanda met him downstairs and helped him carry the boxes up.

"Erica misses you," he said as they walked up the stairs.

"Why do you say that?"

Lawrence followed her into the living room. "When you were up there, it was the calmest I've seen her in years." He smiled as he set his box on the floor. "You were a good influence on her."

"I would have loved to have stayed longer," she said. "But the contract was over."

"Of course. So, what are you up to now? Any big plans?"

"Well, I have a few shifts lined up at the Obsidian."

"Dancing?"

"Yeah."

"Good for you. Are you going to keep writing?"

Amanda hadn't thought about it. "What I did wasn't writing. I was just a research assistant."

"Yes, but you were good at it. Do you keep a journal?"

She shook her head. "No."

"Maybe you should start. If you keep working at the Obsidian, you're going to wind up with a lot of good stories."

*That's true. I'm already off to a good start. I wouldn't believe some of them were real if they hadn't happened to me.*

"You know something, you're right. Maybe I will." Amanda looked at him. "And when are you writing your memoirs, Larry? I know you've got stories of your own, even if you'll never share them with me."

Lawrence smiled. "I actually started writing last week. I've already got ten thousand words."

"That's wonderful."

"You inspired me with all of your prying. So thanks for that."

"Excellent. So, when do I get to read it?"

"You'd look at it?"

"I'd love to."

Lawrence beamed. "I'd love to hear what you think. Let's stay in touch, Amanda. You've still got my number, right?"

Amanda nodded. "Sure do."

"Cool. Well, now it's back to Trent Manor with me. Miss Erica is having guests this evening and I'm driving up to Seattle to pick them up."

"She sends you all over the place, doesn't she?"

"It's all part of the job. I'll see you later, Amanda."

When her phone rang a few hours later, Amanda had just sat down to dinner. She recognized the number as Vivian's and picked up quickly.

"Hello, Vivian. How are you doing?"

"I'm so glad you answered, Amanda. Not good at all, honestly. I was just notified that Jessica Frost intends to sue me if I publish *The Secret History*. Can you believe the nerve of that woman?"

"That's terrible. What are you going to do?"

"Well, there's no way I'm backing down now. That woman doesn't scare me."

"Do you think she's bluffing?"

"It doesn't matter if she is. I'll still beat her." Vivian paused. "What are you doing this evening, Amanda? Do you have plans?"

"No, not really."

"Wonderful. Why don't you come down to the Lounge for a few hours? I have someplace I'd like to show you."

"Sure." Amanda stared at her bowl of spaghetti. "I can be there in half an hour."

"Better yet, I'll send my driver. See you soon."

Ivy wasn't at the door, but the other girl let Amanda walk right in. She found Vivian at a small table in the corner and joined her.

"Thanks so much for coming down," Vivian said. "Clara is out of town and I didn't know who else to call."

"I'm glad to," Amanda said. "I'm really starting to like this place."

Simone walked up. "Can I offer you a drink, Amanda?"

"Thank you. I'll take a vodka-7."

Simone smiled. "I'll be right back, love."

"I have such great staff," Vivian said. "I really am very lucky."

"I can tell they love working here. Especially the dancers."

"I try to treat my staff the same way I would like to be treated." She took a sip of her drink. "Although, thankfully, I haven't had to work for anyone else in a very long time."

"That's quite an accomplishment," Amanda said. "I wish I could say the same."

"You worked as a waitress before Erica found you. Is that right?"

Amanda nodded. "I did. All through college and for a few months after that. Student loans didn't cover all of my tuition, and I still had to eat."

Her drink came, and she took a sip after thanking Simone.

"Can I ask what you studied?" Vivian asked

"Mainly English, actually. I'd still like to do something with my degree someday. It's just that the job market is so terrible right now."

"So, you're overeducated and underemployed? That's terrible, Amanda. Unfortunately, I see it all the time with my dancers." Vivian looked across the table at her. "Tell me, how much of the Lounge have you explored so far?"

"Well, I've seen the offices. And the Water Room."

*Should I tell her about going upstairs? Maybe she knows already.*

"And one room on the second floor."

Vivian laughed. "Oh, yes. Clara mentioned your evening with Miss Spencer. That was quick thinking on your part."

"You're not upset?"

"Not at all. If anything, I admire your ingenuity." Vivian took another sip of her drink. "So, you've never been up to the third floor?"

"I didn't know there was one."

"Oh, yes. It's only used for private parties. I'd be happy to give you a tour." She smiled. "That is, if you're interested."

"It sounds great. I'd love to see more of the Lounge."

"Wonderful, come with me. You can bring your drink."

As they walked past the back-stage Amanda waved at Ophelia, who winked as she continued sliding down the pole. She followed Vivian through the back and into the elevator.

Vivian swiped her pass card and entered a code. They went up two flights and the elevator door opened. The hallway was silent and dark before the motion-activated lights turned on.

"There were no reservations this week," Vivian said. "It's a shame this floor isn't being used more often."

"What usually happens up here?" Amanda asked.

*I mean, I have some ideas.*

Vivian smiled. "How about if I show you? I call this one the Platinum Room. There's a lot of history here."

Amanda followed her into the enormous room. Couches and beds were stationed in various spots. A projection screen took over an entire wall.

"The nice thing about this room," Vivian said, "is that it's soundproof. Patrons can be as loud as they want, and they usually are."

"How interesting."

"Our clients come up here for private times." She paused. "Do you remember the sitting machine on the second floor? Clara mentioned that you quite enjoyed your time on it."

Amanda nodded and smiled at the memory.

*The Uber-Sybian? How could I forget?*

"Well, we have one up here as well. Why don't I arrange another demonstration?" Vivian walked to the couch and sat down. She took out her phone and hit a button. "Roxanne, please send Ophelia to the third floor. Yes, we're waiting."

She turned to Amanda. "I come up here sometimes when I need time away. The stress of running the Lounge has gotten so much worse in the last few months. Now I get this news about Jessica Frost. I just need to take my mind off it for a while. Do you understand?"

Amanda nodded.

"Of course you do," Vivian continued. "I know people see me as a successful business owner. And it's true. I've done extremely well for myself. But it hasn't always been this way. Did I ever tell you I was an orphan?"

"I had no idea. I'm so sorry."

"No, I never had anything handed to me." She gestured around the room. "Everything you see here, everything downstairs, I have earned it all with my hard work. And it could all be taken away so easily. I'm scared, Amanda." She shifted closer, so that her leg was touching Amanda's.

"It will be okay."

"I hope so. The Obsidian Lounge is my dream."

The door opened, and Ophelia entered. She must have come directly from the stage, because all she wore was a top, a short skirt, and heels.

"Thanks for joining us," Vivian said.

"Of course, Miss Starr. I'm sure what you have planned is much more interesting than my usual evening. How should I begin?"

Vivian pointed at the Uber-Sybian, and Ophelia beamed. "Really? Oh, it's been a while. What a treat. I'm on it." She winked at Amanda again as she walked past. "Literally."

"You two must have met the other night," Vivian said.

"Ophelia was wonderful," Amanda told her. "She helped me so much."

"I'm sure she did. Ophelia has always been one of my favorites." Vivian scooted closer, and Amanda felt the weight of her thigh on hers. It felt delightful, and she eased into it, their skin touching. Vivian smiled and held her hand.

"Ophelia, we're ready now."

Ophelia stripped naked, hopped on, and flipped the switch on its side. As the machine hummed to life, she eased down while plucking her nipples.

"I've always loved this one," she said. She smiled at the women on the couch. "It hits all the right spots."

"This room has so much history," Vivian told Amanda as they watched. "I was so wild when I was younger. You know, a few of the stories in the book are about me." She smiled. "I've had some great nights up here. It's been too long."

She pulled Amanda's hand toward her. Amanda went with it, gently petting her lap.

"Tonight is wonderful, too," Amanda said. She turned her hands sideways and guided it between Vivian's thighs, moving up slowly. "Thank you for the invitation."

"I didn't want to be alone. Not tonight."

"I'm here for you."

Vivian gasped in delight as Amanda's fingers teased her. They gazed together at Ophelia, who was grinding away across the room, a look of pure bliss on her face.

"Beautiful, isn't she?" Vivian asked.

Amanda nodded. "Very."

"It's an honor to have seen so many young women over the years pass through here. It's one of my favorite parts of owning the Lounge. That, and access to all the facilities, of course."

"We love you too, Miss Starr," Ophelia called.

"You're so sweet." Vivian turned to Amanda. "I'm so glad you wanted to come up here with me tonight."

"And what do you want?" Amanda asked.

Vivian smiled. "Just touch me."

Amanda reached under Vivian's skirt and squeezed her thigh, then slid her fingers under her panties and felt her wetness.

"Should I stay up here?" Ophelia called. "I'd love to go another round."

"Yes, please," Vivian said. "I'm enjoying the show."

She found Vivian's clit easily and rubbed in swift strokes. Vivian moaned and leaned forward.

"You really know how to touch a woman," she said.

"Shh. Relax and let me take care of you."

Vivian closed her eyes as her orgasm built. She shook softly on the couch. Amanda let her hand lie on her mound for a moment, then slowly pulled it back.

"Okay, Ophelia. You can come down now."

Ophelia hopped down and joined them on the couch. She was naked except for her boots, and her shaved pussy was glistening and wet with juice. "Here I am," she announced. "Where would you like me now?"

"Amanda has been so good to me," Vivian said. "I think she is deserving of a little pleasure, wouldn't you say?"

Ophelia smiled slyly. "Oh, definitely. I hope you enjoy the show. We'll put on a good one for you."

"I have no doubt of that." Vivian slid her skirt off, then her panties. She tentatively stroked herself, then began to massage her clit. "You always do."

Ophelia fell to her knees in front of Amanda. "Now I'm going to do something I've been thinking about all week."

"Oh yeah?" Amanda replied. "What's that?"

"Licking that amazing pussy of yours." She slowly spread Amanda's thighs open and Amanda felt a burst of pleasure deep in her core.

"You're ready for me, aren't you?"

Amanda nodded. "So ready."

Ophelia kissed the inside of her thighs, making her way toward Amanda's pussy. Amanda closed her eyes and gave in to the sensation as Ophelia found her spot. She tensed in anticipation as Ophelia found her rhythm.

She felt a presence and opened her eyes. Vivian had moved closer.

"I'd like to kiss you, Amanda," Vivian said. "May I?"

"You don't have to ask, Vivian."

Vivian nibbled on her lips, then darted her tongue in her mouth. Amanda tensed again as Ophelia continued to lick.

Ophelia turned her head and smiled at Vivian. "Would you like a little taste, Miss Starr? You look like you might."

Vivian shook her head. "No, I couldn't."

"Of course you could. She's waiting for you." Ophelia licked her lips. "Come down here and help me with her, Miss Starr. We can make her come together."

"Please," Amanda murmured.

"This is so unlike me," Vivian said as she moved down to the floor.

"You don't want to miss this," Ophelia said. "Trust me."

Amanda leaned in, savoring the sensation as the two women took turns licking her. Her orgasm built.

"It's so good," she moaned. She closed her eyes as she came, squeezing her legs together. When she opened her eyes, Vivian and Ophelia were kissing on the floor. She joined them, inching toward Ophelia.

"It's your turn now," she told Ophelia. She turned to Vivian. "You don't mind, do you?"

"We can make an exception this time," Vivian said. "She looks too delicious."

"It's time to return the favor," Amanda said. She spread Ophelia's lips with her tongue, then moved up and pressed hard on her clit. Ophelia squirmed with delight.

Vivian watched from the floor and rubbed herself. "Twenty years in the business, and I never tire of this."

Amanda continued to rub Ophelia's pussy. "Watch," she told Vivian. "See how wet she is? She's so close."

"I see."

"Come with her," Amanda said. She heard Vivian's moans as they climaxed together.

Afterward, Amanda took a Lyft home. It was nearly midnight, but Diane was still up watching a horror movie in the living room.

Diane pointed to a bottle of wine on the table. Amanda got a glass from the kitchen and poured a small one.

"How was your day?" Amanda asked. "You do anything special?"

"Not really. Celeste wanted me to let you know she has an audition at the Obsidian on Monday."

"Really? That's great."

"Yeah. I'm going to go down and cheer her on."

"That's so cool. I think she'll fit in there. Everyone's great. I'll introduce you to Sapphire and Ophelia. You're going to like them a lot."

"But will they like me?"

"Of course." Amanda rubbed her arm. "You're adorable."

"I'm not really like them, though, am I?"

"Well, neither am I."

Diane scoffed. "Sure you are."

"What do you mean?"

"You just make it work. You're so confident"

"I don't feel confident."

"You'd never know it."

Amanda smiled. "You're sweet."

Diane shrugged. "I'm just telling you the truth." She took a sip of wine. "You're different since you came back from Trent Manor. Working on that book was good for you, I think. You seem more comfortable with yourself." She frowned. "Not that you weren't before. That's not what I meant."

"I know what you meant. I can feel it, too."

"I'm glad you're back, Amanda."

"Me too. I'm even glad to be back in this shitty apartment."

Diane laughed. "It is pretty shitty, isn't it?"

Amanda looked around the living room at the tan walls and cheap furniture. "The worst."

They looked at each other and laughed, then clinked their glasses together in a toast.

Amanda scrolled through her phone until she found Ruth's number. She smiled as she remembered her last shopping trip and sent a quick text. A few moments later, her phone buzzed. She slid her finger up to answer.

"I'm glad you called," Ruth said. "So you didn't forget about me?"

"Of course not. I've just been so busy with everything. The book project was major, but it's done. Finally."

"Congratulations, Amanda. You must be so relieved. So, what are you up to now? Any plans?"

"Well, I just got back from a few days in New York City."

"Ooh, you were living the glamorous life! You'll have to tell me all about it."

"I'd love to."

"Maybe over drinks?"

"Sure." Amanda paused, an idea occurring to her. "Actually, what are you doing today?"

"Not much. Just laundry day. Why? Do you need help picking out clothes again?"

Amanda laughed. "That's exactly what I had in mind. Are you down? Lunch is on me."

"Amanda, what would you do without me? All right, it's a date. Meet you downtown in a couple of hours?"

"Cool. I'll see you soon."

After a light meal of falafel sandwiches and iced tea at the food carts, Amanda and Ruth strolled up Stark St.

"Okay, where are you taking me?" Ruth asked. "I can tell you have someplace you want to go." She paused. "Someplace special, maybe?"

Amanda smiled mysteriously.

"Ooh, I know. We're going to Legends. Good call."

"I thought you'd like that. I'm going to need your expertise."

"Well, this is definitely in my wheelhouse."

"I know." Amanda opened the door and let Ruth in. The cashier, Tara, was behind the register looking at her phone. When she saw them, she smiled and stood up.

"Hey you," Tara said. "Nice to see you again." She turned to Ruth. "So, how did you like your present? I made sure she got the best one in the store."

Amanda blushed. "Oh, that was for my roommate. This is my friend, Ruth."

"What present?" Ruth asked. "You got someone a present here? Amanda!"

"It was nothing," Amanda said.

Tara smirked. "Whatever you say. So, what are you in the mood for today? More toys? I have more suggestions." She looked back and forth between Amanda and Ruth. "Plenty more."

"Actually, she asked me to help liven up her wardrobe," Ruth said. "Sexy, but also a little classy. She's got a new job dancing."

"Oh yeah?" Tara's eyes lit up. "Where can I see you?"

"I'm at the Obsidian," Amanda said.

"Ooh, nice. I haven't been there forever. Such a cool place. I'll have to come in some night, if you'll be working." She walked across the room, a bounce in her step. "I have a few outfits in mind that will be great for you. This way, ladies."

She led them through the store and into the back room. Rows of lingerie, corsets, and leather skirts were displayed on the walls.

"I don't know where to begin," Amanda said.

"Of course you do." Ruth pulled a few pairs of fishnet stockings off the rack. "Start with these. You're going to want them."

Tara pointed at a black leather top in the corner. Small silver studs surrounded a dark red heart, dead center. "How about that one?" she asked. "Do you like it?"

"Gee, I don't know. It's pretty Goth. Do you think I could pull it off?"

Tara smiled. "Girl, you'd look great in anything."

Ruth nudged her. "Get it, definitely. Go big."

"That's a yes," Tara said. "Let me take it down for you."

"All right," Amanda said. "Let's do this."

Amanda swiped her pass card in front of the sensor at the employee entrance and the door opened.

"It's cool if I come in this way?" Ruth asked.

"Sure, it's cool." Amanda pointed straight ahead. "The bar's right there. This is easier than through the main entrance."

She led Ruth across the floor. It was a busy night at the Obsidian and Ophelia was dancing on the South stage.

As she walked past, she heard her name called out. Ophelia waved them over and walked to the edge of the stage. She gave Amanda a hug, then turned to Ruth.

"You brought a friend tonight," she said. She smiled seductively. "Are you going to introduce me?"

"Of course. Ophelia, this is Ruth. I wanted to show her where I work."

"I guess you could call me her fashion consultant," Ruth said.

Ophelia laughed. "That's great. Amanda needs a little help in that department." She turned and stretched her leg out toward Amanda. "I'm just teasing, darling."

"No, I deserve it after the other night."

"Well, wait until you see what we brought with us," Ruth said. "We picked out some treasures."

"Fantastic," Ophelia purred. "I can't wait to see them. I know Sapphire's around somewhere. She'd love to play dress-up with you again. And so would I." She turned back toward the stage. "Let me finish up this set and I'll come back and find you two."

"I'm going to get changed," Amanda said to Ruth. "I have to be on stage soon."

"I'll grab a drink. Then I'll come back and watch the rest of Ophelia's set." Ruth leaned in and whispered in Amanda's ear. "Thanks for getting me in tonight. You're the best."

Amanda smoothed her skirt down and looked at herself in the full-length mirror in the dressing room. It was a simple outfit, not as fancy as the other two Ruth had chosen for her, but it accented her breasts perfectly and was so comfortable.

Sapphire reached from behind, put her arms around her, and squeezed. "You look stunning, doll. Are you ready to go?" She gave Amanda a quick kiss on the cheek.

"I think so. Having my own outfits makes a huge difference."

"There are plenty of girls in rotation tonight. Saturdays are always busy. You'll probably only get two or three chances up there, so keep your ears peeled. If you don't make it in time, they'll just go on to the next one on the list."

"I will. Thanks."

Sapphire squeezed her again. "You're going to be great."

Sapphire was right. The crowd loved her, throwing their bills on the stage and applauding loudly. She remembered what Ophelia had shown her and found that the moves came naturally.

After the first song, she noticed Vivian walking across the club, a determined look on her face. Clara followed close behind. They found seats on the far side of the stage. After Amanda made her rounds, she danced over to them.

"I'm so glad you came out," she told Clara. She leaned in and rubbed against her softly.

"I didn't want to miss you," Clara said.

Amanda turned her attention to Vivian. "How are you tonight?"

Vivian frowned. "Not good, Amanda. Not good at all." She shook her head. "I can't believe this."

Clara leaned in. "We got bad news. Jessica Frost is threatening to block the publication of *The Secret History*."

"That woman doesn't have a case," Vivian proclaimed. "She'll get laughed out of court."

"Oh no," Amanda said. "What are you going to do?"

"My publishers advised me not to release it. Can you believe them? What cowards." Vivian leaned back in her chair. "I'm not scared. She can bring it. My book is coming out tomorrow, whether she likes it or not." She smiled. "There are already over fifty thousand pre-orders. It's going to the top the charts." She sipped her drink. "And now we wait."

Amanda beamed as she finished her first set. She collected the bills covering the stage, stuffing them into the clutch she had brought for this exact purpose, before grabbing her clothes and exiting the stage. Ophelia gave her a wink as they passed each other, and Amanda winked back.

Ruth had made her way from the bar back to her seat in the front row, and Amanda joined her.

"What do you think?" she asked.

"I love it," Ruth said. "You're really friends with all these girls?"

Amanda laughed. "Yeah, most of them."

"That's so cool." Ruth paused. "Do you think you could introduce me to Ophelia?"

"Oh, sure. She's awesome."

Just then, Ophelia walked up to them. She wrapped her arms around Amanda and kissed her on the cheek. "I watched your set. You were great."

"Thanks," Amanda said. She pulled Ruth close "Ophelia, there's someone I want you to meet."

The next day was Sunday, and Amanda let herself take a leisurely morning. The rain came down steadily, in typical Portland fashion. It was a perfect day to stay inside, and she stretched as she walked to the kitchen to start coffee.

Diane woke up around ten, padding out to the living room in pajama bottoms and a Ramones t-shirt.

"Do you want to get breakfast delivery?" Amanda asked. "My treat."

"That sounds awesome," Diane said. "Where were you thinking?"

"I've always wanted to try that bougie place that opened up on the corner. I forget what it's called, something and something."

Diane laughed. "Ha, you always talk shit about that place."

"True. But they probably make a killer breakfast sandwich."

"Oh, you know they do. Sure, I'm in. Get me one of those fancy smoothies. You know, the green one."

"You got it."

Diane had the day off as well. When the food arrived, they ate together on the couch. They finished their coffee, and Diane made a pot of black tea.

Amanda gathered their wrappers and threw them back in the paper bag. She stood up to throw it away and felt her phone buzz. It was a text from Clara asking her to call. She hit the phone icon and Clara picked up on the second ring.

"Well, it happened," Clara said.

"What?"

"She didn't listen to them." Clara gave a deep sigh. "I thought Vivian was smarter than this."

"Slow down and start at the beginning. Is this about *The Secret History*?"

"Yes. She published it, like she said she was going to. And it's a massive hit. Top ten on the New York Times." Clara sighed. "Go see for yourself. It's all over the internet."

"What's going on?"

"There's been an injunction against the Lounge, and Jessica is suing Vivian for ownership. Apparently, there's an old contract that Vivian never told anyone about. Maybe she forgot. But Jessica still has an ownership stake in the club. And she's suing for libel. Vivian could lose everything."

"There's no way. How is that even legal?"

"She was waiting for this. She'd already drawn up the papers. As soon as the book came out, she pounced. It's bad." She took a breath. "This is a takeover."

"Well, shit. What's she going to do?"

"She has two choices. Either close the OL now, or it can remain open. With Jessica Frost in charge." Clara paused again. "I know she won't close. We'd all be out of a job, and Vivian won't let that happen. Until this is settled, we have a new boss." She paused again. "What are you doing tonight?"

Amanda looked over at Diane, who was sipping tea. "Just hanging out with Diane. We don't have any plans."

"I could really use some company right now. I don't know what it's going to be like at work tomorrow, and I'm kind of freaking out about it. Can you come over? I have wine, and we can order takeout or something."

Amanda moved her mouth away from the phone. "Hey, do you want to go over to Clara's?"

Diane shrugged. "Sure, sounds like fun."

Amanda smiled. "You can count on us."

The Lyft dropped them off at Clara's. She lived in a condo in the West Hills, not far from their apartment.

She greeted them in a pink t-shirt and black tights. Her hair was down, and Amanda could tell she had been crying.

*Poor girl. She's really freaked out.*

"Thanks for coming over, guys," Clara said. "Let me take your coats. Would you mind taking your shoes off?"

"Of course not," Amanda said.

"Thanks." She waved them in. "There's wine in the fridge, and I'll order food in a bit. Let me know what you want." She frowned. "I don't have much of an appetite."

They set their shoes by the door and walked into the living room, which was larger than Amanda and Diane's entire apartment. Tasteful prints decorated the walls, and a large stereo sat next to a 60" flat-screen.

"Do you live by yourself?" Diane asked.

Clara nodded. "This is what you can afford when you're Vivian Starr's assistant. I've had a good run."

"Well, it's a great apartment. I'm not even going to ask what you pay."

Clara gave a slight smile. "Don't. I don't know how I'm going to afford it when I'm unemployed. I'll probably have to get a roommate."

"It's a two-bedroom?"

"Yes. I use the spare bedroom as an office."

"Well, sharing a place isn't so bad." Diane looked at Amanda and smiled. "If you find the right person. Someone you're comfortable with. But I'd love to live by myself eventually."

"Really?" Amanda put her hand on her hip. "This is the first I'm hearing about it."

"Nothing personal, Amanda, you're awesome. But the two months you were up at Trent Manor were kind of incredible. I could get used to it."

"It does have its advantages," Clara said. She walked to the kitchen and returned carrying a bottle of white wine. "Who wants a glass?"

"Me, me," Diane said. She studied the label. "Ah, you have the good stuff."

Clara smiled. "When you work with Vivian, you develop a taste for it. She taught me so much about the finer things in life." She poured three glasses and handed them around. "I wish it wasn't raining. I'd love to sit out on the balcony and look at Forest Park."

"I don't know. I like it inside," Amanda said. "Your place is so cozy."

"Come on, I'll give you a tour. You can bring your drinks." Clara led them down the hall. "You've seen the kitchen and the living room. There's a bathroom at the end of the hall across from the spare bedroom. Here, I'll show you the upstairs."

The carpeted stairs felt soft against the soles of Amanda's feet.

*Luxury. I've never had a place this nice besides Trent Manor. And that was never really mine.*

Her bedroom was just as Amanda had imagined it - clean, spacious, and organized. A few rows of books sat on wooden shelves, and fine art prints graced the walls.

"This is my room," Clara said.

"You have two bathrooms?" Diane exclaimed.

"I know, it's kind of bougie. After all, I can only use one at a time. It's pretty nice, though."

"I can't even." Diane turned to Amanda. "Can you imagine if we had our own bathrooms?"

Amanda nodded. "That would be a game changer."

Clara flipped a switch, and the lights turned on outside. Amanda joined her at the sliding glass door, and they looked toward the distance together. Greenery went on as far as she could see.

"It's incredible," Amanda said. "It's like the whole forest is your backyard."

"It's a great place to relax in the summer," Clara told her. "I have parties sometimes, just a few girls from the club. You should both come next time."

"We'd love to," Amanda said.

"I haven't had company in a while," Clara said. "Thanks for coming over."

"Of course." Amanda took a sip of wine and set her glass down. "We all need a friend right now."

Clara turned to her. "I do. I really do. This is all so stressful." She leaned in, and Amanda held her tightly as she sobbed.

"It's okay, Clara," she said. "Let it out. I'm here for you."

"You're such a good friend." Clara wiped her eyes on her sleeve and turned to Diane. "I'm sorry. I don't know what's wrong with me. I'm not usually this emotional."

Diane moved closer and rubbed her shoulder. "It's okay."

Clara reached out and touched Diane's hand. "Thank you. I feel so silly now."

"No way," Amanda said. "There's nothing wrong with having feelings."

Clara sighed. "I know, but I usually keep it together better than this."

"We're all friends here." Amanda sat down and put her arm around Clara. "You don't have to keep it together around us. We've all been there."

"I know. Thank you, Amanda." She leaned in and snuggled against Amanda's neck. "Wow, you feel really good."

Amanda reached around and massaged Clara's neck. She felt a large knot on the right side and pressed down.

"You're so tense. This thing at the Obsidian is really getting to you."

Clara nodded and let her chin fall. "Yes. I don't want to think about it anymore."

"We can help you with that if you want. Lean back and relax. We'll take care of everything." She motioned to Diane, who sat on the other side of the bed.

Clara leaned back on her pillows. "Like this?"

"That's perfect. I want to show you one of the techniques I learned from Dee. I think it might help you."

"I'll try anything at this point," Clara said.

Amanda turned around on the bed and faced Clara, then rubbed her neck, easing the tension away.

"That feels so good."

"I think I'm doing it right, but I'm not sure. I've only ever had it done to me once."

"Whatever you're doing, it's working."

Amanda motioned for Diane to sit down on the other side of the bed. "Will you help me with her?"

"Sure." Diane inched closer. "What do you want me to do?"

"Start with her feet. The feet hold a lot of tension."

Diane nodded. "It's true. My feet have been killing me lately."

Amanda smiled. "Well, I'll just have to do you next. But let's start with Clara."

"Of course." Diane slowly peeled Clara's socks down and rubbed her ankles, then her feet.

"You two are spoiling me," Clara said.

"Oh, we're just getting started."

Clara removed her shirt and set it on the end of the bed.

"You read my mind." Amanda leaned in and gave Clara a soft kiss on the forehead. "Loosen up and let go. Be in the moment with us."

Diane scoffed. "You sound like such a hippie, Amanda." She moved her hands up Clara's legs and softly rubbed. "Where did you learn this stuff, anyway? Your massage friend?"

"Yes, Dee," Amanda said. "I had such a profound experience with her." Amanda thought back to her Tantric afternoon at Casa Sirena and smiled. "She's coming to the Lounge to visit me tomorrow. She said she has exciting news."

"Why doesn't the Obsidian have a massage therapist for the staff? That's a great idea." Clara sighed. "I guess it's too late now."

"Put it all out of your mind." Amanda continued to knead Clara's neck, moving down to her shoulders and pressing hard. "Everything will be waiting for you tomorrow, but you'll be able to deal with it better if you're relaxed. Today, let us take care of you."

"Okay." She shifted on the bed. "That feels amazing."

"We're just getting started," Diane said. "Amanda's not the only one with techniques."

Clara smiled. "Is that so? Have you been holding out on us?"

"I only know a couple of things." Diane slowly rubbed Clara's stomach, then slid her hand down. "But I'm very good at them. You seem like you're ready to learn."

"I am." Clara stretched back further on the bed. "This is just what I needed."

Amanda leaned in and gave Clara a soft kiss on the mouth, then let her lips wandered down her chest. "I love this." She gave Clara's nipple a lick and felt it harden against her tongue.

*Wow, she's so responsive.*

Diane slid Clara's panties off and stroked her with her fingertips. She licked her fingers and pressed softly against Clara's clit.

"That feels so good." Clara spread her legs wider and clasped her thighs invitingly. "You have such a gentle touch, Diane."

"I'm easing you into it," Diane told her. "Just wait."

Amanda rubbed Clara's shoulders. "Diane can get kind of wild."

"Is that true?" Clara asked.

Diane nodded. "You're going to find out."

Amanda continued to rub, breaking up the knots as Diane slid her fingers across Clara's clit. "You carry so much tension, girl. Just let go of it."

"I know," Clara said.

"Let it all out." Amanda moved to the head of the bed and pressed down on Clara's hips as Diane fingered her to orgasm.

"Fuck," Clara cried out as she came, then laughed. "That was amazing. You two are just what I needed."

"Oh, we're just getting started," Amanda said.

Diane smiled at her. "You're next, girl. Come down here and give me a taste."

Amanda took off her top and pants and laid down next to Clara. Diane moved into position, licking the inside of her thighs and making her way up. She found Amanda's clit and teased it gently.

"You're already so wet," Diane said.

"I can't help it. Watching you two was so hot."

Clara turned over and faced Amanda. She gave her a soft kiss on the lips. "Thanks for coming over."

"Of course...ooh!"

Diane twirled her tongue around Amanda's clit and ran her hands across her ass. Amanda moaned and reared up as Clara licked one nipple, then the other. Amanda's orgasm built.

"That's fuckin' teamwork," Diane sang out to Clara.

*Leave it to Diane to make a Tenacious D reference. My God, these girls are going to make me come so hard.*

Clara kissed her hard on the mouth, swirling her tongue against hers, which sent her over the edge. She moaned as she came, then relaxed on the bed, savoring the moment. Her core pulsed with the release, and she grinned to herself.

She slowly sat up and put her arm around Diane. "Okay, you're next."

"Wonderful," Diane said. "Show me your stuff."

"You want to help me out, Clara?" Amanda slid her hand down Diane's side, softly tapping her with her fingers.

"Definitely."

Amanda looked into Diane's eyes. She seemed at peace, defenses down. Amanda smiled.

"What is it?" Diane asked.

"Oh, nothing. You just look so content right now."

"I'm just relieved."

"What do you mean?"

"I thought it would be weird. You know, sharing you like this." She reached across and took Clara's hand. "But it feels right."

"I'm glad," Clara said. "I feel the same way."

"I'm so happy," Amanda said. "I wasn't sure what was going to happen." She licked her finger and swirled it around Diane's nipple. "But I know what's going to happen now."

Diane gave a delighted squeal and spread out on her back. Amanda moved over to let Clara in and slid her hand across Diane's thigh.

"I want to watch you lick her," she told Clara.

*I can't believe this is happening.*

"Gladly," Clara said. She scooted in and kissed the inside of Diane's thigh, then inched her face closer. She opened her mouth and kissed Diane's pussy.

*Lovely. I think I'll give Clara a little treat. She deserves one.*

Clara's ass was in the air, and Amanda crawled behind her and softly cupped her cheeks. Clara tensed up for a moment, then Amanda felt her relax. She crouched down and licked her cheek. Clara scooted back, and Amanda planted her face between Clara's cheeks.

"Mmm," Clara moaned, her voice muffled and her head bobbing up and down.

Amanda felt Clara's asshole contract as she explored with her tongue. Making quick strokes, she edged further, then reached around and slid her finger along Clara's pussy.

*She's so wet. I love it.*

Amanda slid two fingers inside and rubbed Clara's clit.

"Fuck, don't stop," Clara said. "Please."

Amanda continued to lick and felt Clara's orgasm build. Clara and Diane came at the same time and sank into the bed together, and Amanda smiled to herself.

*What a great way to spend the afternoon. We'll have to do this again soon.*

When Amanda arrived for her shift the next evening, Sapphire was at the bar holding a drink. It was a normal Monday night at the OL, but things felt different. Heavier. Somber.

She walked up to the bar and gave Sapphire a long hug.

"I guess you heard," Sapphire said. "The Frost regime starts tomorrow." She sighed. "I'd say I hope things won't change too much, but who am I kidding? Of course they will. They always do." She took a sip of her drink. "This sucks so hard."

"It won't be the same without Vivian."

"No, it won't. And the Frosts are going to come in and mark their territory. It always happens."

Amanda nodded. "I'm just going to keep my head down. Jessica will definitely remember me from the interview."

"Clara, too."

"Yeah."

Sapphire set her empty drink on the bar and stood up. "I need to get ready. You want to help me choose my first outfit?"

"Sure. Then you can help me."

"Cool, let's do this. Damn it, let's have a good night."

Amanda felt much less nervous on stage. A round of applause greeted her as she made her way to the pole. Looking out at the crowd, a sense of power flowed through her.

*I'm think I'm getting the hang of it. I could really start to like this.*

She saw a familiar face in the front row and walked over to Dee.

"Hey, Amanda," Dee said, looking a little out of place at the club. She wore a light green dress and small gold nose ring.

"You finally came," she said. She sat down and pulled up close. "I'm so glad you're here."

"I've wanted to come here for a long time," Dee said. "Thanks for inviting me." She looked up at Amanda and set a five on the stage. "This is what I'm supposed to do, right?"

Amanda laughed. She nodded as she brushed the bill aside with her foot. "Yes, exactly. And keep them coming." She winked. "Thank you, dear." She wrapped her legs around Dee's head and moved in closer.

"I get it. I provide a service as well," Dee said. "In fact, that's what I came to tell you. Do you have time to catch up between your sets tonight? There's so much happening right now. You're going to love this."

"Definitely. Hang out for another song and we'll get a booth in the bar. I want to hear all about it." Amanda gave a shake of her breasts and stood up.

"I'll be right here," Dee said.

Dee ordered a cranberry and soda for herself, and a gin and tonic for Amanda. She paid for their drinks, and they sat next to each other in a booth in the corner of the bar.

Amanda took a sip of her drink. "So, what's your big news you can't wait to tell me?"

"It's so exciting, Amanda. I'm opening a massage and yoga studio."

"Really? That's amazing! I'm so happy for you."

"I know." Dee beamed. "I can't believe it's really happening. Everything just fell into place. It feels like the right move."

"Where are you going to be?"

"I got a great deal at a studio in the Pearl. It's a little funky, but I can make it work. I'm in town this week to sign papers. And celebrate, of course!"

"Thanks for sharing the news with me."

"When I found out I was moving to Portland, I knew I had to call you."

"I'm glad you did. Moving is always tough. I can't imagine starting a new business at the same time."

"Yeah, I took on a lot. But I'm ready for a change. Casa Sirena was good to me, but it's time for me to strike out on my own. Luckily, I'm bringing a lot of my clients with me."

"Really?"

Dee nodded. "Oh, yes. All the women I've met over the years. Now they won't have to drive to the coast to see me, they can just come to my studio. I'm already taking reservations for next month."

"That's wonderful."

"Right? My biggest problem right now is finding people to work. My friend Melanie is the only instructor I have so far. I'll need a couple more full-time employees once everything gets going. If you know of anyone, let me know."

"You're the only massage therapist I know," Amanda said. "But I'll ask around."

"Thank you."

"And of course, I'll be your first customer. I still have so much to learn."

Dee smiled. "Very true. I'd love to continue your personal training. We can even start before the Lotus opens, if you want. I'll be in town full-time starting next week."

"That's the name of your studio? The Lotus?"

"Do you like it?" Dee took out her phone and opened Instagram. "You want to see the new logo?"

"Of course." Amanda moved closer to see. Her thigh touched Dee's, and she smiled. She let it stay there as they looked at the pictures together. A small painting of a yellow lotus flower on a light green background.

"I love how it turned out," Amanda said.

"Melanie is an awesome artist. She's making a sign for the window, and this design will be on all our cards."

"This is so cool." Amanda took out her phone and sent a quick text. A response came back quickly, and she smiled. "Back at it. Got to run."

"So soon? Didn't you just get off stage?"

Amanda leaned in and smiled. "I asked to get my stage shows over early so we can spend some time together. I just have one more rotation, then we can do whatever we want." She stood up. "Come watch me again, then I'm yours for the rest of the night."

"Really?"

She smiled and held out her hand. "Come on. I'll get you get a front-row seat again."

Amanda's second set went even better than her first. Her confidence grew each time she took the stage, the moves coming more naturally all the time.

*Sapphire and Ophelia were right. All it takes is time and practice.*

She made her way to the side of the stage and made eyes at a small group of women. They laid their bills down and she scooped them up and shoved them toward the center of the stage, then turned back and gave them a wink.

She noticed a new arrival on the other side of the stage and sashayed over. The woman was gorgeous, her short dark hair cut professionally in a bob. She wore an expensive black dress and smelled like money.

*Let's see who this is. I look the look of her. Maybe I can squeeze in a private dance. Dee will understand.*

Amanda leaned down and whispered in her ear. "How are you tonight, love? Enjoying your evening?"

"I'm glad I came down," the woman said. "It's nice to finally see the place."

"Oh? Is this your first time at the Obsidian? Let me welcome you."

The woman nodded. "Yes. My aunt has told me so much about it, though. I believe you met Jessica Frost a few weeks ago." The woman leaned back in her chair. "She certainly remembers you, Amanda. You made quite an impression on her."

*Jessica Frost. Oh, wow. It's already starting.*

"Yes, we've met."

"I'm Gina," the woman said, holding out her hand.

Amanda thought a moment before accepting it. When she finally did, the sparks flew.

*Wow. I liked that a little too much. I need to be careful. Remember, she's the enemy.*

She composed herself. "Hi Gina," she said. "So, what brings you down?"

"I felt it was important to meet the staff before I arrive tomorrow in my more official capacity."

"I see."

"Don't worry, Amanda," Gina said. "It will be a smooth transition. I promise." She smiled, displaying her perfectly white teeth. "You have nothing to worry about. I don't plan on making any major changes." She looked around the room. "At least, not right away."

Amanda stood up. "It was nice to meet you, Gina. Excuse me. I need to make my rounds."

"Of course you do. The customers here have refined tastes, and it's important to remember that." She smiled. "I've been watching you, Amanda. You've got something special. I hope you'll be happy here for a long time." Gina winked. "I'll see you again soon."

Amanda walked away, shaken.

*Why does she have to be so damn sexy? I want to hate her for what she's doing, but it's so hard when she looks like that.*

She felt Gina's eyes follow her as she gripped the pole and took a spin.

*This is way too much pressure. I swear, this set can't get over soon enough.*

She pulled her skirt up and gave the ladies in the front row a peek, then spun again.

*Just a few more minutes. I can do this.*

"Yes, I saw her walk in," Dee said. "I could tell she was important. Something about how she carried herself. She's your new boss?"

Amanda nodded, then took a sip of her drink. They had ended up back at their table, where Dee bought her another drink.

"Gorgeous lady," Dee commented. "A knock-out."

"Good genes, I guess. I've seen pictures of Jessica back in the day. She was a hottie."

"Still, they're making bad karma for themselves with this takeover." Dee paused. "I know you don't believe in that stuff, Amanda."

"I don't know," Amanda said. "I mean, think you get what you give in life. In general." She took a deep breath. "I'm going to be honest, that interaction kind of fucked me up. I wish I had a cigarette."

"Amanda, you don't smoke."

"I know. I quit a couple of years ago."

"Well, don't start again now. I have a much better idea." Dee leaned in and brushed against her. "Aren't there private rooms available?"

"There are." Amanda smiled and pushed her drink away. "Are you thinking what I'm thinking?"

"That's why I'm here."

Amanda led Dee through the bar. Ophelia was on stage, and she glanced at her, then into the audience. Gina was still in the front row, watching Ophelia intently.

*I see she's making the rounds. Probably trying to decide who she's going to get rid of first.*

She tried not to think about Gina Frost, but the memory kept intruding.

*I know I shouldn't want her. But...*

She reached for Dee's hand. Dee took it and held it, firm and calm.

They made it to the elevator. Amanda swiped her pass card, and they got out on the second floor.

"You've really never been here before?" Amanda asked. "Not once?"

"I always heard stories from the women at Casa Sirena. It sounded like something I should experience for myself."

"It is." She pointed at the four doors. "These are the Element Rooms."

"Fire, Water, Air, and Earth. I see. Do you have a favorite?"

"I've only been inside the Water Room, but it was wonderful."

"Then let's go there." Dee smiled and squeezed Amanda's hand. "Water is soothing, and I sense you could use some soothing right now."

"I really could."

The light above the door was green. Amanda swiped her pass card again and entered her code on the panel.

"They're serious about security here," Dee remarked.

"Yes. It used to be a lot wilder back in the day, apparently. But yeah, access is pretty restricted." Amanda pointed at the camera above the elevator. "Clara told me the cameras are just for show. They never look at the footage unless there is an issue."

"Do you believe her?"

"Yes." Amanda opened the door, and Dee followed her inside.

The Water Room had been cleaned recently. The couch and table were freshly wiped down, and there was a faint ocean scent, like ozone and salt. A mild breeze flowed down from the ceiling, cooling Amanda's forehead.

"Ooh, I like it in here," Dee said.

"Right?" Amanda sat on the couch and breathed in slowly. She closed her eyes, then exhaled. She felt Dee's presence next to her and reached for her hand. Dee squeezed back, and they sat for a moment in comfortable silence.

Finally, Amanda spoke. "This was a great idea. Thank you for suggesting it."

Dee put her arm around her, cradling her. "Remember, you can always choose to start your day over. Any time you want."

Amanda laughed. "That sounds like more of your mysticism."

"Laugh all you want, but it works." Dee turned to her and looked into her eyes. "By holding on to negative feelings, the only person you hurt is yourself."

"I guess you're right."

"Do you think Gina is still thinking about your conversation? Letting it take up valuable real estate in her head?"

Amanda thought about it. "Actually, she might be."

*You don't know how she looked at me. Like she wanted to take me right there.*

"Okay, maybe she is. But will worrying about it change anything?"

"I guess not."

"That's right. So don't waste your energy on it." Dee rubbed her shoulder and brought her in closer. "Instead, you can channel it into something positive. I have a few ideas."

Amanda pulled her in tight. Dee was soft and warm, and she nestled next to her. "You know, you're a smart woman."

"I learned so much from my Master, Swami Kamananda. She taught me ways to control my mind." Dee smiled. "And body. Yoga gives you focus, it really does. I'd love to teach you what I know. We can pick up where we left off at the coast."

Amanda thought back to their encounter in the massage room at Casa Sirena and a surge of desire flowed through her. "Yes, I'd like that."

Dee moved her hand up to the back of Amanda's neck and squeezed. Amanda winced.

"Let's take care of the big problem first."

Amanda rolled her neck in a small circle and felt it crack. "I'm in bad shape, aren't I?"

"I've seen worse. But you could be doing a lot better."

Amanda gave a sheepish grin. "I know."

"Self-care is a revolutionary act. Always remember that." Dee stood up. "I'm going to give you a demonstration. Take off your shirt and lie down on the couch."

"But this is your night," Amanda said. "This was supposed to be about you. You're my guest."

"There's plenty of time. Trust me, you'll feel so much better."

Amanda took her shirt off. She knew she was safe with Dee.

*We connected so fast. It's amazing.*

The blue light and sound of the ocean relaxed her, and she sank into the couch.

Dee began to massage her shoulders. "Have you been doing the exercises I suggested?"

Amanda shook her head.

"I didn't think so." Dee pressed harder and pushed down, easing Amanda's tension away. "This won't go away on its own. You need to be proactive."

"I know," Amanda said. "It's just that it's always something. First, I stressed myself out making sure *The Secret History* could be published on time. Now there's all this mess."

"You're never going to be in a place where everything is perfect and you have all the time you need to take care of yourself. It's just not going to happen. You need to make time for it." Dee continued to press, pushing outward and releasing more knots. "Prioritize yourself, Amanda. You're worth it."

Amanda sighed.

"I won't stay away so long next time. I promise." Dee made her way down Amanda's back and pressed down on her hips. "There's little pockets of stress everywhere. Most people just carry it in a couple of places. You're all over the place, girl."

"Go big or go home, I guess?"

"Joke about it all you want, but you're setting yourself up for trouble down the road. I'm serious. You need a routine. You need structure and discipline."

Dee gave her hips a hard shove, and Amanda felt them realign. All her tension vanished in an instant.

"Wow. That was amazing. What did you do?"

"That's another trick I learned from Kamananda. Do you feel better?"

"I feel wonderful."

"That technique creates an energetic shift." Dee lifted her hands away. "You can sit up now."

Amanda sat up, her bare breasts exposed. The pressure from the couch and Dee's touch had made her nipples hard. "Now, how about that dance?" She stood up and faced Dee. "I should do something nice for you."

Dee smiled. "Well, okay. Honestly, I've been curious about these private dances for a while."

"I still can't believe you've never been to the club."

"I was always busy with school or work. Getting my massage license took most of my energy. And I never had many friends. I never connected with most of the other therapists at Casa Sirena." She smiled. "But I always heard stories about the Obsidian Lounge and knew I wanted to come here."

"And now you're going to get the full experience." She pointed to the couch, and Dee sat down. Amanda placed a foot on each side and slowly ran her hands up her thighs. "Leave everything to me. I want to try some of my moves on you. The ladies really seem to like this one." She leaned in and slowly slid down the front of Dee's dress.

"I see why. You use your body like an artist."

Amanda beamed with pride. "Really? Thank you."

"Definitely. I see why they wanted you to work here. You have a special way about you that's so seductive."

"I'm just winging it up there most of the time." Amanda slid down Dee's body. "I've learned so much since I started working here."

"I knew you were fun the moment you got on my table."

"Well, I was pretty riled up that day."

"Oh, really? Why is that?"

"Do you remember Erica?"

"The beautiful dark-haired woman you came with? Of course. How could I forget Erica?"

"Well, we shared a moment just before we came in. In the shower."

"Just a moment, huh?" Dee smiled slyly.

"Yes, but she got me really worked up."

"I could tell. But, of course, that's easy to do." She slid her hand across Amanda's lap. "You're already wet, girl. Feel."

Dee reached for Amanda's hand and guided it downward. Amanda felt her dampness.

*Wow, she's right. Hee hee.*

"Does dancing usually arouse you like this?"

Amanda nodded. "It does. I love the feeling of power it gives me."

"I see. Well, go ahead. Let me see some moves. I've been waiting for this."

Amanda leaned in and slid down Dee's body, her breasts touching. She reached around and hugged Dee's hips. "You feel so good. I'm going to make this one extra special."

Dee spread out on the couch and touched her thighs, then let her hands stray up. "I'm so ready."

Amanda pounced on her, grabbing her ass and grinding slowly.

Dee sighed and softly bit her lower lip. She traced her fingers around her nipples, and Amanda noticed how hard they were.

She stood up and shook her hips provocatively. "I'm still figuring out my moves." She took a deep breath, held it, then slowly exhaled.

"You're a natural," Dee told her. "Why don't you come back here?"

Amanda smiled and dropped to her knees.

"Not yet," Dee told her. "Take your time. There's no hurry."

"I can't help it. This is just so hot."

"Control yourself. Remember my lesson on the massage table."

Amanda smiled, thinking back on her strong, extended orgasm under Dee's guidance.

*I'll never forget it.*

"It's just difficult when you're so-"

"I know." Dee lifted her dress, showing her panties. "I feel it, too. But keep going. Give me some moves, show me what you've got. You promised me the full experience."

"I did, didn't I?" Amanda stood back up. "Well, I usually start like this." She swayed back and forth, letting her hips lead her. She reached up and traced her hard nipples.

"Okay, stop."

"What?"

"Amanda, what are you feeling right now? Pay attention to your body. What is it telling you?"

"I don't know."

"So? Concentrate until you do. If you go into every encounter the same way, you miss out on many of the subtleties." Dee spread her legs wider. "How am I feeling right now? Focus on me for a moment."

Dee smiled mysteriously, but she wasn't hiding anything. Completely open and receptive.

"You're horny."

Dee laughed. "Of course. What else? Go below the surface. Find the truth of the situation."

"Is this more of your spiritual wisdom?"

"Maybe. But it's also practical. Just try it."

Amanda closed her eyes and concentrated.

"No. Not like that. You don't have to struggle to figure it out. Let the truth of the moment reveal itself to you."

"You want me to touch you?"

"Very good. But where?"

Amanda sat down and let her hands wander to Dee's hips. "Right there."

"Now you're getting it."

She continued to press, kneading with her palm and making her way down to Dee's thighs. The side of her hand brushed between Dee's legs.

"Yes, right there. That feels wonderful."

Amanda worked Dee's hips, then crept toward her center. She made slow passes, getting closer each time. She waited until she knew Dee was ready, then slid her hand on the inside of her thigh and softly stroked her outer lip with her finger. Dee moaned and spread her legs wider.

"Healing is sexy," Dee said. "It's what I'm going to teach at the Lotus."

"I can't wait for my first lesson." Amanda sat down and continued to rub, escalating the intensity.

Dee smiled and covered Amanda's hand with hers. "Slow down. Are you ready to learn? I'll show you something. Just a taste of what you can expect."

"Of course." Amanda felt Dee's pulse throb in her hand, her pussy hot and wet. "Teach away."

"What's the longest you've ever held an orgasm?"

"Held it? What do you mean?"

"The build-up to the climax." Dee pushed Amanda's hand slowly into her. "How long does it usually last?"

Amanda thought about it. "I don't know. Once I get going, I just want to come. I don't think about it, I just let it go."

"Then let this be a lesson to you." Dee guided Amanda's hand, showing her how she wanted to be touched. "Pay attention. Be aware."

*No problem there.*

Amanda felt as Dee's orgasm built.

"Slow down," Dee murmured. She seemed stable and focused, her breath strong and constant. "As slow as you can. Feel the change. Feel what happens."

Amanda touched her nub, pushing up with two fingers. She sensed Dee's breath speed up.

"I could go like this for hours," Dee told her, and smiled. "Or I could come any time. It's always up to me."

"What do you want to do?" Amanda chuckled. "In the moment."

"Take me," Dee told her.

Amanda sensed every motion as Dee came. She watched as she closed her eyes and shuddered, a look of pure bliss on her face.

*Amazing. I so need to learn how to do this.*

Dee slowly opened her eyes and gazed up at Amanda. "I can teach you how to do it," she said, as if reading her mind. "I think you'll find it very enlightening."

Amanda gently brushed Dee's hair back. "I'm looking forward to more fun times at the Lotus."

Amanda and Dee held hands as they took the elevator down and back to the lounge. Amanda grabbed her backpack from the dressing room and they walked outside to Dee's car.

"We should get tea next week," Dee said. "I know everything's going to be stressful, and I'd love a friend."

"That sounds great. When's the big opening?"

"Well, we're going to have a soft opening on the first to break the space in. Just me and Melanie and few of her friends. You should come."

"Do I need to bring anything?"

Dee touched her shoulder. "Just yourself." She paused. "A water bottle. And wear comfy pants, there's a lot of stretching involved."

"Ha, no problem there."

"I'm going to have a free beginner's class once a week. To give back to the community. If you know of anyone who might be interested, let them know."

"I will."

"And who knows? Maybe I can talk you into giving a pole-dancing workshop sometime."

Amanda blushed. "Oh, not me. You want Sapphire or Ophelia for something like that."

"Would they be interested?"

"Maybe. I'll ask."

"Wonderful." Dee gave Amanda a kiss on the cheek and opened her car door. "I'll call you next week."

Amanda scowled as the car icon crawled across her phone screen. It paused on the corner a full minute before gradually resuming its journey.

*Great. I'm going to be so late. Just what I need today. Come on, come on.*

A notification suddenly flashed: **We found you a closer driver.**

She clutched the bag with her two outfits for the night and her heels.

*Thank God. I really should have bought a car with the money I saved working for Erica.*

Her face fell as she considered the large sum coming out of her account the next day for rent.

*It'll be okay. I still have some savings. If I can sock away a bit more working at OL, maybe I can get something cheap.*

**Your new driver arrives in four minutes.**

Checking the time, she made a quick calculation. She just might make it on time after all.

She breathed a sigh of relief as the new driver pulled up. Four minutes could make the difference between walking into work right under the bell or being late on her first day with Gina as the new manager.

"Obsidian Lounge, please," she said as she climbed into the backseat.

"Rough day?" The driver glanced at Amanda in the rearview mirror with a kind smile as he merged into traffic.

"Yeah, you could say that. I appreciate you getting here so quick."

"No problem. I'll get you there as fast as I can."

Amanda settled in for a quick journey. She closed her eyes, took a deep breath, and visualized walking into the club with time to spare.

Ivy stood at the entrance, letting a long line of customers in two and three at a time. Amanda adjusted her bag on her shoulder and speed-walked over.

Ivy smiled and opened her arms for a hug. "Amanda! I'm so glad you're here. I wasn't sure if you were going to show up."

"Really? Why wouldn't I?"

"Oh, you must not have heard yet. I figured Clara told you. A bunch of girls walked out last night. Allegiance to Vivian, you know?"

Amanda nodded. "Wow. That bad?"

"They thought so. I don't know. Gina has been okay with me so far." Ivy shrugged.

"I guess I'll find out for myself soon enough. Look, I've got to get in there. I hope your night goes well, Ivy."

"Thanks. You too," Ivy said. She gave Amanda a shy smile. "Maybe I'll see you around later."

Amanda blushed. "You know where I'll be."

"Okay, now in with you. Don't keep them waiting." Ivy held the door open for her. "Go knock 'em dead."

Amanda trudged inside, her heart sinking at Ivy's news. With so many dancers gone, she knew the ones who were left would have to work twice as hard. She also knew her checking account wouldn't let her follow them out the door.

She steeled herself, hoping Gina might be a reasonable boss. And if not, that she could at least stay off her bad side.

The familiar sounds of the club surrounded her, pounding music and laughter. There was an edge of chaos in the air, as if nobody was steering the ship. The room was only half-filled, and no one was at the bar.

Sapphire waved to Amanda from the stage. Amanda waved back before making her way to the dressing room.

When she walked in, she froze. Usually, there would be several girls changing or applying their makeup, but not tonight. Outfits and boots were scattered everywhere, rather than arranged by performer like Vivian always liked them.

Amanda sighed.

*They must have torn through everything in anger when they left. This is gearing up to be one hell of a shift.*

She changed from her street clothes into her first outfit of the night, stowing her bag in her locker. She heard the door open and turned her head. Gina stood for a moment before entering. "Hi, Amanda."

"Hi," Amanda said, smoothing down her sleek black dress and turning her focus back to touching up her evening makeup.

Gina let the door swing shut behind her with a click. She stood for another long moment, looking at Amanda with an odd expression.

"I suppose you're wondering what all this is about," she finally said, breaking the silence.

Amanda paused, lipstick half applied. Keeping her gaze fixed steadily on her reflection, she responded neutrally. "It had crossed my mind."

Gina moved closer, her floral perfume filling the space between them. "I know change can be hard. But like I said before, you have nothing to worry about." She placed a manicured hand lightly on Amanda's shoulder. "I promise I won't do anything drastic. I respect you girls too much."

Amanda tensed slightly at the unexpected contact. "Well, that sounds good and all..." she began.

"You don't believe me?" Gina asked. She edged nearer until Amanda felt the whisper of her breath. Neither of them moved, although they were almost touching.

Amanda finally turned to look her in the eyes. "It's not just that. This whole situation isn't right. Vivian loved this club. She put everything she had into it."

Gina held her gaze steadily. "I'm sure she did. And I can appreciate that, truly. But it's up to my aunt and I now to decide what's best for the Obsidian going forward."

She pulled over a stool and sat facing Amanda, their knees almost touching. "I didn't plan for this to happen, you know. I didn't have much choice - it was either step in here or go back to waitressing. I'm sure you can understand having to take opportunities when they come your way."

As Amanda studied the vulnerable expression on Gina's face, her defenses lowered slightly. "Yes, I get that," she replied.

"My aunt might own this place now, but she's getting up there," Gina continued, standing up and slowly pacing the dressing room. "She has no idea how to run a huge, busy club like The Obsidian Lounge. That's why I'm asking you for help. I can't do it alone, especially with everyone acting so strangely around me."

Amanda considered her perspective. "The girls are just afraid of the changes. Everything's happening so fast. I'm sure you can understand why they're on edge."

Gina nodded. "Of course. And you're absolutely right. Everyone just needs a little time to settle into the new normal." She glanced at her watch and sighed heavily. "I've got a million things to do tonight. Thanks, Amanda. We'll talk more later, okay?"

With that, she gave Amanda's arm a gentle, reassuring squeeze and slipped back out the door, her heels clicking down the hallway.

Alone again, Amanda finished applying her makeup, lost in thought. Gina seemed sincere about wanting a smooth transition, but it still didn't sit right with her. She set down her makeup brush and assessed her finished look in the mirror. One way or another, this was going to be a long night.

Stepping out on the main floor, Amanda was immediately struck by the lack of organization. The DJ was nowhere to be found, leaving an automated playlist to blast through the speakers. No one was announcing the dancers' sets, either.

*I wonder if she left, too. This is really bad.*

The girls mingling around the floor looked just as lost and confused. Sapphire hurried over to her, brow creased with worry.

"Hey, have you talked to Gina yet?" she asked.

Amanda nodded. "Yeah. I'm still not sure what to make of her. Do you think she's for real?"

Sapphire shook her head uncertainly. "Who knows? So far her management style is a fail." She gestured in frustration at the chaotic, rudderless club. "I mean, how does she expect us to work like this?"

Amanda sighed, feeling the beginnings of a headache coming on. "Jesus. I need a drink. At least we still have a bartender."

"I'll join you," Sapphire said. "Don't worry, we'll get through this."

As they walked past the main stage, Ophelia frantically waved them over. She looked exhausted.

"Amanda, thank God you're here! Can you take over for me? Please? I've been up there for five songs straight and I'm going to lose it!"

She motioned to the empty announcer's booth. "No one's managing anything tonight. It's anarchy. And not the good kind."

"Of course, girl, go take a break," Amanda said warmly, moving to take Ophelia's place on the stage. "I've got you."

"Thank you," Ophelia said, nearly wilting with relief as she shuffled off toward the dressing room.

With Ophelia gone, Amanda took a deep breath to steady her nerves.

*What's going on? This place is falling apart.*

She wasn't prepared when the next song blared from the speakers - some techno remix she didn't recognize.

*It isn't my usual style, but I'm a professional. I'll make it work.*

Putting a smile on, Amanda sauntered out on stage. Her mind was still reeling from everything that had happened, so she called on her muscle memory to mesmerize the crowd with smooth, sensual moves.

Soon, the bills began appearing in the straps of her outfit as she lost herself in the familiar sensations - a needed distraction from all the chaos.

Swaying in time to the beat, she let the music flow through her, electrifying her body. She was in her element again.

When the second song ended, Amanda was surprised to find herself still alone on the stage. No one was coming to relieve her.

With no other choice, she launched into a third number, then a fourth. Her muscles burned with exhaustion, but she kept her smile locked in place, pouring every ounce of energy she had into her movements.

By the fifth song her legs were trembling, barely supporting her as she twirled and dipped through her set. A layer of sweat coated her. This was beyond anything she had ever done before.

On a normal night, a solo stint on stage might last two or three songs max before another girl rotated in. Apparently, the old rules didn't apply tonight. Her job was to stay under the lights and entertain the crowd for as long as possible.

Faint with fatigue, Amanda was relieved when Sapphire finally showed up to take her place.

*Still no sign of Gina providing any leadership.*

"Get down from there. I've got you, girl," Sapphire assured her. "Go get that drink. You deserve one."

With an encouraging smile, she headed back out under the lights, leaving Amanda to sink gratefully into a chair until her next set.

Amanda stepped onto the stage again amid raucous cheers from the crowd, fueled by new fiery energy. The confusion and anger that had built up within her flowed through her movements - making them bolder and even more intense than before.

As she locked eyes with the eager women gazing up at her, Amanda saw her own emotions reflected back at her - raw desire, excitement, intensity. Their hunger sated something deep within, flooding her veins with adrenaline and power.

Hands grasped at her thighs, slipping bills into her stockings as she dipped and swayed inches away from them. Amanda pressed closer, allowing more lingering, teasing contact that elicited impassioned moans and sighs from her audience.

She felt connected to these women in the charged moments of intimate contact and release. This was why she stayed, the fleeting yet electrifying encounters that left her totally aroused.

Song after song passed in a blur as Amanda lost herself in the pounding beat and sensual rhythm. The overworked ache of her muscles barely registered, drowned out by the current of desire coursing between her and the spectators.

Only when exhaustion overwhelmed her did she feel the need to stop and rest. But the insatiable hunger in their eyes called to her own hunger – the need to give them more, to push past her limits just a little further.

Lost in the pulse of the music and the crowd's hungry energy, Amanda was startled when a firm hand gripped her arm. She turned to find Gina beside her, looking both amused and a little irritated.

"It seems like you've got everything under control up here," Gina remarked wryly, shouting to be heard over the throbbing bass. "Why don't you take a break before you start a full-scale riot?"

Amanda looked out into the club. The spectators were on the verge of frenzy after her marathon stint on stage. With a nod to Gina, she retreated behind the curtain as dissatisfied groans rose up, her overtaxed muscles trembling.

Adrenaline still coursing through her body, Amanda made her way through the crowded club toward the bar, where Ivy leaned casually against the counter.

"Girl, you were on fire tonight!" Ivy exclaimed. She handed her a bright blue cocktail and looked her up and down approvingly. "That spin into the chair drop was killer. You really know how to drive them wild."

"Thanks," Amanda replied, sipping the sweet drink as her heartbeat began to even out. She turned toward Ivy, captivated by her bright energy and words of praise. "I wanted to give them a great show," she added with a flattered smile.

"Mission accomplished," Ivy said, her eyes twinkling. She leaned in closer, dropping her voice. "Your performance definitely inspired some thoughts for later," she purred, trailing a hand up Amanda's arm. A new heat ignited inside Amanda at her touch.

"I aim to please," she said.

"Mm, I bet you do," Ivy murmured back. They gazed at each other for a long moment, the wordless connection between them intensifying amid the noise and energy in the club.

Amanda took a sip of her drink before leaning into Ivy, eager to discover where this flirtation would lead. The club was forgotten as they moved closer together. Ivy's fingers trailed up Amanda's thigh, setting her skin on fire.

"I mean it. You were amazing tonight," Ivy purred, her breath tickling Amanda's neck and making her shiver. "I couldn't look away. The way you move...it's captivating."

Amanda turned, taking hold of Ivy's chin to pull her into a passionate kiss. The taste of cinnamon and rum on her lips was delightful, just a little sweet.

Ivy nipped at her lower lip. "Give me a private show, Amanda? Just you and me?" She shifted onto Amanda's lap before Amanda could respond, rolling her hips in an unhurried grind. "I want to go upstairs with you again."

Amanda's hands clutched Ivy's waist, drawing her in. She could feel the heat between Ivy's legs through the thin layers of fabric. With each sway, the pressure and friction grew until they overwhelmed her.

A moan escaped Amanda's lips, muffled by Ivy's fervent kisses. She moved a hand up Ivy's side and over her breast, giving her nipple a soft pinch.

Ivy gasped, arching towards Amanda as her movements sped up. "I want more," she pleaded, her breath coming in quick gasps. "Come on, take me upstairs to one of the rooms. Please, Amanda."

Amanda gladly obliged. She grabbed Ivy's hand, guiding her up to the second floor of the club. Ivy smiled when she saw the door Amanda chose.

"The Water Room again? Oh, you read my mind. I've dreamed of coming back here for weeks."

"It feels right, doesn't it?" Amanda smiled, letting her step inside first. "After you."

Ivy gasped in awe, taking in the lavish space. Dimly lit by flickering faux candles, opulent hues of deep teal and azure glimmered around them. One wall featured an exquisite infinity-edge waterfall, its soothing sounds filling the air. A plush aquamarine couch surrounded a small, raised stage.

"I love this room so much," Ivy said. "I have such good memories of being with you here. I hope they keep it the same and don't ever change anything. It's just so special to me."

Warmth rose in Amanda's chest. She stepped closer to capture Ivy's lips in a tender kiss, savoring their softness. Her hands wandered into Ivy's hair, and she held her close as they undressed each other between lingering kisses and teasing touches.

She gingerly led Ivy to the stage, then set her down on the cushions. Hands and lips explored slowly. The most attention was paid to her tender areas—the dip of her collarbone, the insides of her wrists, the backs of her knees—leaving no spot untouched.

Finally, she settled between her thighs. She planted a gentle kiss on Ivy's slick folds before letting her tongue delve deeper, losing herself in softness and heat and the sweet taste of Ivy's arousal.

Ivy's climax coursed through her body when Amanda finally took her over the edge, her cries of delight bouncing off the walls of the Water Room.

Amanda crawled further up. She knew the night was just beginning, every moment a new opportunity to savor.

Ivy clutched her face, drawing her in for a kiss. "Your turn," she said afterward, nudging Amanda onto her back.

Amanda sighed as Ivy's mouth trailed down her throat to her chest, tongue teasing her sensitive flesh. She arched into Ivy's touch, yearning for more.

Ivy took her time exploring Amanda's body, discovering what made her quiver and gasp. Her caresses were unhurried yet purposeful, keeping Amanda balanced on the brink of pleasure and expectation. By the time her fingers finally slipped between her thighs, Amanda was soaked and trembling.

"Please," Amanda begged, moving her hips up into Ivy's touch in search of relief.

"Patience, love. I want to savor every moment." Ivy bent her head to drop fleeting kisses and gentle licks along the length of Amanda's thigh. Amanda's breath came in quick, shallow pants as Ivy teased her, lips hovering over her skin.

"Please," she implored, writhing on the couch. "Take me. I'm yours."

Ivy caressed her until Amanda was shaking. She met Amanda's gaze, heavy with desire. "Then tell me what you want."

Amanda's hands curled around Ivy's hair, tugging her closer, keeping her in place. The tension increased steadily, but it was not enough.

"Ivy," she said. "I need - I need -"

Ivy groaned, teasing the bundle of nerves at Amanda's center. "What do you need?" She nuzzled Amanda's thigh, tasting skin and sweat. "Tell me."

Amanda growled in frustration. "Ivy!"

Ivy whipped her head up and closed her mouth over Amanda's clit in a kiss, her tongue flicking out to tease. Amanda screamed, bucking up off the cushion. Her fingers tightened on Ivy's arms, pinning her in place as she rode out the waves of her orgasm with Ivy's mouth on her. The tension finally eased out of her.

"I knew you were going to be a delight, Amanda. I love everything about this," Ivy said, crawling up next to her. She traced her finger along Amanda's forehead.

Amanda's heart raced with anticipation as Ivy leaned in again, pausing a moment before pressing her lips to hers. Soft and still tinged with her arousal, they were unbearably sweet. She moaned, arching up to meet Ivy's hand.

Ivy's tongue glided across her bottom lip before diving inside. She straddled her thighs, hands skimming up Amanda's sides to cup her breasts. Amanda moaned as the pleasure surged through her all over again. She cried out, wave after wave rolling through her, stealing her breath away.

Amanda called out Ivy's name, overwhelmed by the intensity that coursed through her.

As the quakes settled and her cries quieted, Amanda drew Ivy into a gentle embrace, their skin flooded with sweat and satisfaction. They kissed tenderly, basking in the glow that surrounded them.

Amanda approached Gina's office the next evening, a knot of anxiety tightening in her stomach. Had Gina seen them last night on the security feed? She steeled her nerves as best she could, unsure what to expect from this unpredictable new manager.

Gina glanced up from some paperwork as Amanda entered, a sly grin twisting her mouth. "Have a seat, Amanda," she said, gesturing to the chair across from her desk.

Amanda perched cautiously on the edge of the seat, her pulse racing as she met Gina's gaze.

After allowing the tension to build for a long moment, Gina continued. "I couldn't help but notice that you and Ivy seemed quite...close last night."

Amanda felt a flush bloom across her cheeks but held Gina's stare. "Yes, we went up to the Water Room for a private show. I didn't think the cameras were on."

Gina let out an amused laugh. "Oh, don't worry. They weren't. But you two weren't exactly discreet when you made your way up there. I saw your little performance at the bar." She paused. "Look, Amanda. I don't have an issue with whatever's going on between you two." Her expression shifted, turning grave. "As long as it doesn't affect your work. We could have used you on stage while you were up there doing who knows what."

Gina leaned back in her office chair, regarding Amanda with an inscrutable expression. She slowly stood up and circled the desk with deliberate, measured steps, then perched on the edge directly in front of her.

Amanda's mouth went dry under the intensity of the stare. Seeing Gina clearly for the first time, she noticed the alluring curve of her hips, the full shape of her breasts. A jolt of heat shot through her body, mingling surprise and unexpected desire and a flutter of apprehension.

*Where is this going?*

Gina leaned closer until she felt the warmth of her breath on her neck.

"We should get a drink together," Gina said suggestively, trailing a manicured finger along Amanda's bare arm. "I'd love to hear your ideas about how we can make the club better. I'd be very open to your... input."

Amanda's pulse leapt, but she hesitated. Getting involved with the boss was treading dangerous waters. But this tempted her more than she could have predicted.

Seeing the conflicted emotions play across her face, Gina pressed closer, taking Amanda's chin firmly in her hand.

"I won't take no for an answer," she said. It was clear this was not a request.

Against her better judgment, Amanda gave in, powerless to resist as raw desire flooded her body. Caution always lost out to temptation.

"Since you put it that way, how can I refuse?" She got up and walked to the office door, aware of Gina's piercing gaze following her. Pausing at the threshold, she glanced back alluringly. "It's a date. Tomorrow night."

As the door clicked shut behind her, Amanda wondered if she would regret what she'd just set in motion.

Amanda slid into the plush booth across from Gina, the dim lights of the lounge casting the table with an amber glow. Two whiskeys sat between them - twin temptations beckoning, though for now Amanda resisted the urge to drink.

She couldn't stop the nervous energy throbbing through her body as Gina's hungry gaze swept over her. This clandestine meeting already felt like a dangerous game.

"I'm surprised you came," Gina said, her eyes glinting knowingly over her glass as she took a slow sip.

"Yeah...me too." Amanda laughed uneasily, the sound barely audible over the mellow jazz. She busied herself adjusting the napkin in her lap.

Gina leaned closer, dropping her voice to a sultry murmur. "Though not unpleasantly so. Seeing you and Ivy last night is all I could think about today. I want a taste of what she had."

A bolt of arousal shot through Amanda at such bold words. She wet her lips nervously, an action Gina's eyes keenly followed.

"This is inappropriate," Amanda protested half-heartedly. "You're my manager." But even as she said it, she felt her reservations crumbling.

"That excites you, doesn't it?" Gina asked as she stroked Amanda's arm. "Admit it, it turns you on." Pushing herself closer, Gina's other hand moved to Amanda's hair and pulled her into a kiss before Amanda could move away.

To her surprise, Amanda returned the kiss passionately. The softness of Gina's lips caused her senses to reel, even as warning bells rang in her head. She was drawn to Gina's touch, casting caution aside. When the kiss finally ended, she was desperate for more.

Taking a deep breath, she met Gina's gaze. "You know we can't do this."

Gina smiled, her expression coaxing and sensual. "But we want to," she murmured, her fingers tracing Amanda's jawline. "Come home with me, Amanda," she said, softly brushing a thumb over Amanda's lips. "I have plans for you."

Amanda leaned into her touch, heart pounding in her veins. She knew if she gave in now, there would be no turning back. Their eyes locked and desire grew heavy, making Amanda forget the reasons why she should refuse. She took a swig of liquid courage, feeling it burn through her body. Then she stood up and took Gina by the hand.

"Show me."

The door shut behind them and they pressed together, their lips meeting and stealing Amanda's breath away. All thoughts of protest drowned in passionate sensation–Gina's soft curves, the nip of teeth on her lower lip, fingers fumbling with her buttons.

A distant voice told her that this was wrong, but Amanda didn't care. She unzipped Gina's dress, desperately wanting to see, feel, and taste more of her. A trail of discarded clothing followed them to the bedroom, where they tumbled onto Gina's massive bed.

Their bodies fit together perfectly, Amanda's slender frame neatly molding against Gina's athletically toned build. Amanda ground herself against Gina's thigh, heat rapidly building between her legs and leaving her yearning for more.

"Please," she begged. "Just take me."

The world faded away. All that remained was Gina's hands on her skin and the rhythm of their bodies moving together in perfect harmony. Amanda's hips jerked with each passing wave of pleasure coursing through her body. She ran her fingers through Gina's hair, bringing their lips together for a passionate kiss.

Gina placed an expertly positioned thigh between Amanda's legs, preventing any escape from their increasing passion. A faint moan escaped Amanda's lips at the pressure, and she clutched onto Gina, her inner muscles clenching desperately. "Gina..."

"Shh..." Gina soothed, her fingers trailing down Amanda's stomach in a trail of fire.

Amanda's head tipped backwards as she rocked against Gina's thigh, the tension coiling within her until she felt like she would explode. She let her hands roam over Gina's body, tracing the dips and curves of each muscle as she trembled underneath her touch.

"Keep going," Gina commanded, a hoarse edge in her voice.

Amanda lifted her gaze to see Gina watching with dark, smoldering eyes. Heat stirred in Amanda's belly as she cupped Gina's breasts and gently teased her nipples.

Encouraged, Amanda smacked her ass and rolled her over on her back. She leaned in for another kiss, stopping any further pleas as she massaged Gina's inner thigh, then slipped two fingers inside.

Gina moaned as Amanda increased the pace of her movements and pressed firmly. She thrusted against Amanda's hand hungrily. Amanda moved to cup one of Gina's breasts and pinched lightly just as Gina let out a cry of pleasure.

Amanda grinned mischievously. "Like that?"

"Oh God, yes." Gina's hips jerked as Amanda's hand traveled lower and lower until she found her hot center again.

Amanda's fingers kept exploring, tracing circles around her slick entrance before slipping inside again. She circled against the walls of pleasure, driving her on.

Amanda moved in a frenzied rhythm, exploring every inch of Gina's body with passionate fervor. Her tongue tangled eagerly with Gina's as she went faster and faster. Gina tensed beneath her as the pleasure built to a crescendo and finally crashed over her.

Amanda gasped for breath as they parted. She rocked forward once more, resting her forehead against Gina's and savoring every second that their skin touched. Gina's hands slid around to cup her ass tightly, urging her closer as her voice emerged in a throaty whisper: "Give me more."

Amanda's breath became ragged as she watched Gina writhe in pleasure. She pressed harder, her vision beginning to blur.

Gina tilted her head back and cried out. Her body arched and hips moved wildly as she climaxed. Amanda continued to use her fingers, coaxing out more intense waves of pleasure from her.

"Please, more," Gina begged. "I want more." Her eyes were manic, pupils dilated with desire.

Amanda maintained an even beat with her hand, pushing even deeper with each stroke. She gave another hard squeeze. Gina gasped and convulsed in her arms, her body spasming as she climaxed a second time. Finally, Gina relaxed in her arms, then slowly withdrew.

"Wow," she said, opening her eyes.

Amanda smiled. "You know, I still have some energy left." She propped herself up on one elbow to admire Gina's flushed skin.

Gina beamed back at her. "That's good, Amanda." Her voice was low and husky with desire. "Because you're next."

Amanda's eyes gleamed at Gina's words. "Well, then." She climbed off and moved to the end of the bed. She turned in place, lifting her ass and tucking her knees under her, then looked over her shoulder expectantly. "I'm all yours."

Gina pressed her lips against Amanda's cheeks, then reached around Amanda's thigh and rolled her over onto her back. Amanda gasped and pressed against her.

She slid her tongue down Amanda's pussy, then up again, teasing her clit. Amanda moaned and arched her back as Gina licked her cunt in slow, teasing circles. She dipped her tongue inside and Amanda's moans grew in intensity as Gina sucked harder. She pulled back, dragging her tongue against the folds of Amanda's pussy, then gave a long, slow lick up her wetness.

Amanda moaned as Gina flicked her tongue rapidly against her pearl of flesh.

Gina felt the spasm and tasted the sweet tang on her lips. She gave one last flick and Amanda gave a wild shudder as she climaxed.

Amanda's heart pounded in her chest and sped up with every step she took toward the Earth Room. It had been two months since she had left her job with Erica Trent, but it felt like a lifetime ago. She hadn't expected to come face to face with her former employer so soon, let alone provide a private dance for her.

*When Erica Trent wants something, she gets it. And I guess tonight she wants me.*

Her heels clacked against the floor as she stepped cautiously into the dimly lit room. It smelled musky and sweet at the same time, like sweat and dust and sex. A coy smile played on her lips as she spoke, soft in expectation of being heard only by her audience of one: "Ms. Trent. Fancy seeing you here."

Erica raised her head from her drink, vaguely posed like a queen on her throne. Her gaze roamed over Amanda's body as if searching for a secret only they shared. She chuckled low in her throat, thick and throaty. "I wasn't sure you would see me." Her fingers glided along Amanda's jawline. "I was foolish to ever let you go."

A shiver of longing ran down Amanda's spine as she looked into Erica's deeply captivating eyes. "I don't belong to you anymore, Miss Trent," she said, holding her gaze.

Erica chuckled again and leaned forward, bringing her in for a scorching kiss.

For a moment, Amanda relished the warmth and familiarity of Erica's touch - letting herself be dragged in again by her powerful spell.

Erica smirked with satisfaction. "Now, why don't you show me what you've been learning during your time at the Obsidian," she said. "I'm sure you've learned many new tricks."

The prospect of playing this dangerous game sent a surge of adrenaline through Amanda's veins. The urge to explore Erica's body again was impossible to deny. With a courageous breath, rose to her feet, then took a step forward.

Steadying her posture, Amanda glided into her routine, swaying to the captivating rhythm and encountering Erica's gaze with a sly smile.

*Fine. I'll give her a dance she'll never forget.*

She shimmied and twirled, her leather-clad body undulating to the beat as Erica watched longingly. Erica moved closer, her hands wandering over Amanda's curves before gripping her hips and pulling her down onto her lap.

"I didn't say you could touch," Amanda scolded.

"You didn't have to, dear." Erica's fingers flexed possessively on Amanda's hips. "Your body tells me you're exactly where you want to be." She scooted back, giving her room to look Amanda in the eye. "You can keep fighting if you want, but we both know how this is going to end. After all, you always enjoy it more when I'm in control."

Before Amanda could respond, Erica captured her lips in another kiss. Her tongue pushed forward, and Amanda grabbed her shoulders for support amidst the swirls of pleasure flooding her body. She knew she should pull away, but desire won out. She returned the kiss with passion.

When they separated at last, Amanda moved against the thigh that had snaked between her legs in search of satisfaction.

Erica let out another low chuckle, followed by a sultry whisper. "That's my naughty girl. I haven't even started yet, and you're already moving on me like a wild animal. Do you see now what you've been missing all this time?"

She gripped Amanda's ass, forcing her to move faster. The pleasure made Amanda sigh and cling to her for support. She knew it was part of Erica's tactic to break down her defenses, but her body responded as if programmed to obey her touch.

"Good girl. That's perfect. Just as I remember you."

Amanda clung to the familiar contours of her ex-lover's body, alarms going off in her mind while still wanting more. Erica had always been Amanda's weakness, and tonight reminded her why. If she couldn't find the strength to pull away, the battle was lost already. And when Erica's hands roamed possessively across her skin, craving overwhelmed her defenses.

A hunger within urged Amanda to embrace her with all her might. When Erica explored deeper, she gasped with pleasure. She had forgotten how talented Erica was with her hands, and the potent effect of being the center of her attention.

Erica eyed Amanda curiously. "You don't have any objections, do you? You're obviously free to leave at any time. "

Amanda shook her head. She knew it was pointless to contradict her. Erica urged Amanda up and off her lap, tightly gripping her hand as they fell onto the soft rug together. Amanda gasped as Erica settled atop her, pinning her in place. Grasping Amanda's wrists with one hand, she raised them over her head.

"Now then," Erica purred, her free hand lazily skimming down Amanda's side. "Whatever shall I do with you?"

Amanda's breath hitched in anticipation, her pulse racing as Erica's fingers lingered near the zipper of her leather top.

Erica stared down at her, eyes alight with hunger and mischief. "I think I'll start by removing this."

She trailed the zipper down in a languid glide, peeling the top open to expose Amanda's bare breasts. A rumbling sound of approval escaped Erica's throat as she leaned down to kiss Amanda's throat and collarbone. She curled a finger around Amanda's silver necklace.

"Exquisite. I believe this one came from my collection. Did you wear it especially for me?"

Amanda gasped, her back arching up as far as Erica's grip would allow. "Yes—I mean, no—I just..."

Erica laughed. "Shh. No need to explain." Her hands roved down to Amanda's bare shoulders, then over them to cup her breasts. "I always appreciated these most of all."

Amanda stifled a moan as Erica's thumbs drew circles around her taut nipples in a steady rhythm. She grabbed hold of Erica's shoulders, her nails digging into the fabric of her blouse.

"Erica, please," Amanda begged, pushing into Erica's touch.

"Please what, darling?" Erica gave a gentle nip to Amanda's collarbone, causing her to cry out softly. "You'll have to be more specific." Her fingers tormented Amanda's nipples with a tight pinch.

Amanda whimpered as her hips moved in search of friction. "Touch me," she begged, not caring how desperate she sounded.

"Mmm, since you asked so nicely." Erica glided down Amanda's body, leaving tantalizing kisses in her wake.

Amanda clenched the rug with her fists. Her thighs spread wider, and Erica's hands slid up her legs. She brought her hands back down to Amanda's hips, then lifted them slowly to the top of her leather leggings.

"May I remove these?" Erica asked, her voice low and rough in Amanda's ear.

Something about the way Erica asked made Amanda's heart beat faster. She was exposed, completely at Erica's mercy. Amanda nodded, unable to find her voice.

Erica's fingertips brushed against the inside of Amanda's thighs, sending a jolt of need through her. "Shh," Erica soothed, stroking Amanda's cheek. She brushed Amanda's hair out of her eyes and planted a soft kiss on her forehead. "Relax. You know you're in good hands."

Amanda jolted as Erica's fingers brushed against her.

"So wet for me already," Erica murmured, tracing her fingers up and down Amanda's slit. "You're almost dripping."

Amanda blushed, a warmth spreading through her chest at Erica's words.

Erica chuckled, pressing a kiss to the corner of Amanda's mouth. "Just how I remember you in the hotel in Vancouver," she said before kissing her deeply.

Amanda moaned into the kiss. Erica's fingers were only inches away from where she wanted them. She brought her hands to Erica's hips, gripping her hard.

Erica broke the kiss and trailed her lips down Amanda's neck. She circled her fingers around Amanda's clit, and Amanda moaned into Erica's ear.

"Please, Erica," Amanda said, her voice quivering. "I need you."

Erica's answering moan vibrated against Amanda's neck. She slid her fingers inside, her touch firm, yet gentle.

Amanda rocked her hips, pushing into Erica's touch. She squeezed her eyes shut, trying to delay the explosion she felt building inside her.

"You've missed this, haven't you?" Erica asked, tracing circles around Amanda's clit.

Amanda released a shaky breath. "Yes," she said, her voice barely above a whisper.

Erica slid her fingers in deeper, and Amanda gasped.

"Are you going to come for me now?" Erica asked, her voice husky. "Come for me, Amanda. I want to feel you."

Amanda bit her lip, nodding. She moved her hips faster, trying to get more friction.

Erica's thumb replaced her fingers, and Amanda cried out as she pushed into her.

"Fuck yes," Amanda panted. She shut her eyes as the sensations overwhelmed her. "God, Erica." She let out a soft moan as her orgasm built. She tried to hold back, but Erica's touch, combined with her words, was too much.

"Come for me now, Amanda," Erica said. "Be my good girl."

Amanda let out a broken moan, her orgasm washing over her. Her fingers gripped Erica's hips as she rode out the waves of pleasure.

Erica moved up to embrace Amanda during her tremors. Amanda clung tightly, pressing her face into the curve of Erica's neck.

Eventually, Amanda pulled away. She stood up and slowly got back into her outfit.

Erica watched intently from the rug, her hair disheveled and blouse half-unbuttoned. "Do you have to leave so soon?" Erica pouted. "I thought we would continue at my place. It's been far too long since I've had a guest at the Manor. Sylvie is only good for so much."

Amanda swallowed hard, shaking her head. "I should really get back to the floor now. I'm sure they need me on stage."

Erica moved towards Amanda, her hands cradling her face. "Don't tell me you're done with me already," she said. "We were just getting started."

Amanda gasped in surprise, wobbling slightly as Erica released her. "Erica," she said firmly. "Your time is up, and I need to go."

Erica sighed impatiently and stepped back. "You're so uptight, Amanda. Alright then, off with you. But I don't think this is the end of it. You'll come back to me soon enough."

"We'll see about that, Miss Trent," Amanda replied tersely.

Amanda staggered out of the Earth Room, her legs unsteady, her face flushed. She leaned against the wall, taking a few deep breaths as she thought back to the hunger in Erica's gaze.

*She's right. This isn't over. Not by a long shot.*

Footsteps echoed down the hallway and Amanda hastily attempted to fix her mussed hair. Gina came into view around the corner and a queasy feeling filled Amanda's stomach.

"Well, well," Gina said as she stopped in front of Amanda. "Looks like you had quite an eventful dance. When Erica Trent requested you personally, I knew I should have expected trouble."

Amanda straightened her shoulders and held Gina's gaze firmly. "I had everything under control in there," she replied carefully.

Gina moved closer, towering over Amanda in her heels. "Did you? It seemed to me that Ms. Trent was the one calling the shots."

"Hold on a minute. You were watching us?"

"Of course I was." Gina smiled. "It's just one of the many privileges of running the Obsidian."

"How dare you." Heat flooded Amanda's cheeks, but she maintained eye contact, determined not to back down. "It might have looked compromising, but I know my limits."

Gina raised an eyebrow challengingly. "Do you?" Reaching out, she tilted Amanda's chin until they stared directly into each other's eyes.

"Come down to the office with me, Amanda. We need to talk."

"Okay, fine."

Amanda followed Gina numbly down the elevator, then down the hallway to her office, dread settling like a weight in her stomach. She perched on the edge of the leather chair, her muscles tense, as Gina settled behind the desk.

"I'm disappointed in you, Amanda," Gina began, her voice sharp. "Getting overly friendly with the clients is a bad look for all of us."

Amanda frowned, confusion breaking through her anxiety. "Come on, Gina. You know our private dances get intimate sometimes. All the girls do it. Don't single me out."

Gina's eyes flashed. "Maybe that was the way things were under the old management. But I'm rebranding The Obsidian Lounge as a more upscale establishment. No more of this behavior."

"That's bullshit, and you know it."

Gina's eyes narrowed. "Watch your tone with me, Ms. Jones. I'm your boss now, and I will not tolerate insubordination."

She rose from behind the imposing desk and strode toward Amanda, her heels clicking menacingly on the hardwood floor. Amanda fought the urge to shrink back into her chair as Gina loomed over her.

"As a matter of fact, I don't believe you have what it takes to work at a high-class establishment like the Obsidian Lounge,"

Gina continued, her voice dripping with contempt. "Your judgement is clearly lacking if you think behavior like that is acceptable." She placed her hands on the arms of Amanda's chair and leaned in close, her floral perfume overwhelming Amanda's senses. "Your pathetic lack of self-control with someone like Erica Trent just shows me you don't have the discipline required."

"Unbelievable," Amanda said. "You're really unbelievable, Gina."

Gina abruptly pushed off the chair and turned her back on Amanda. "Get out of my sight before you embarrass yourself any further. Go clean out your locker. You're done here, Amanda."

Amanda remained frozen for a long moment, stunned speechless. As the initial shock wore off, the truth dawned on her. This dressing down had nothing to do with club policies or reputation. Gina was just jealous that Amanda had not chosen to remain exclusive with her. This was about punishing her for finding pleasure with someone else.

Amanda rose to her feet, resentment and hurt welling up within her.

Without a word, she strode from the office, her head held high. She maintained her composure as she gathered her belongings from the locker room, ignoring the curious glances of the other girls.

The night air was crisp but welcoming as Amanda emerged from the club's front entrance. She paused on the sidewalk, closing her eyes and inhaling deeply, then pulled out her phone and requested a Lyft.

Amanda dragged her feet as she walked down the hallway to her apartment, the weight of the evening's events bearing down on her shoulders. She fumbled with her keys, nearly dropping them before managing to unlock the door.

Stepping inside, she was greeted by the comforting familiarity of her modest living room. Diane glanced up from where she was curled on the sagging couch, a book open on her lap.

"You're home early. Rough night?" Diane asked, setting her book down and standing up.

Amanda sighed and shuffled over to collapse onto the couch cushions. She let her purse slip to the floor with a thud and nodded. "You could say that."

Diane's frown deepened at her uncharacteristic silence. "Do you want to talk about it?" she asked gently. When Amanda didn't respond, she went to the kitchen and poured two large glasses of red wine. She pressed a glass into Amanda's hand before settling back onto the couch, angled toward her friend attentively. "Take your time."

Amanda took a long sip of wine. Keeping her eyes downcast, she finally said, "Gina fired me. Claimed my behavior was 'unacceptable' and would ruin the club's reputation."

"That bitch. Obviously she doesn't know anything about the club."

"Yeah. It started when Erica Trent requested me for a private dance," Amanda said.

Diane nodded, all too aware of Amanda's and Erica's history. "Well, she sounds like a real piece of work," Diane said. "I'm so sorry." She gave Amanda's shoulder a gentle, comforting squeeze. "Try not to dwell on it too much. It's their loss. She's going to chase everyone off and run the club into the ground."

"You're right," Amanda sighed, draining the last of the wine from her glass and setting it aside with a dull thud. "It doesn't make it any less frustrating, though. I was really starting to enjoy dancing." She shook her head, leaning back into the lumpy couch cushions. "I'll figure something out. I always do."

"Yeah, you will," Diane told her. "And I'll be with you."

Amanda smiled. "Thank you. Please tell me that isn't the last bottle of wine."

Morning light streamed in through the living room window as Amanda settled on the couch, phone in hand. She took a deep, steadying breath before dialing Dee's number.

The line clicked after a few rings. "Amanda! I'm so happy you called," Dee said warmly. "We're counting down the days until we open the Lotus. It's all happening so fast!"

Amanda smiled, instantly put at ease by Dee's cheerful voice. "That's wonderful. I know how hard you've worked for this." She hesitated briefly. "Hey, do you still need another instructor?"

"Of course! I'd love to have you on board. Your experience will be invaluable," Dee responded enthusiastically. "When can you start?"

Amanda exhaled in relief, the last of the tension easing from her shoulders. "How about tomorrow? My schedule just opened up unexpectedly," she said wryly.

Dee laughed knowingly. "You need to tell me this story. But absolutely, their loss is my gain. Come by the studio this afternoon and I'll buy you lunch. There's still so much to do before opening day. I can put you to work right away."

"You're a lifesaver, Dee. Thank you so much."

"Don't worry about a thing. I'll personally oversee your training and get you up to speed. It will be a pleasure. And I do mean a pleasure. Just get down here, girl."

Amanda set the phone down with a smile and got up to get a cup of coffee. Dee's support and compassion were exactly what she needed right now. With her positive influence, maybe this unexpected twist wasn't an ending after all, just a fresh beginning down a new path.

# Also by Jasmine Bishop

**Gaia's Garden**
Gaia's Garden Episode 1


**The Obsidian Lounge**
The Obsidian Lounge Episode 1
The Obsidian Lounge Episodes 1-5
The Obsidian Lounge Episodes 6-10
The Obsidian Lounge Episode 10


**The Takeover**
The Takeover Episode 1
The Takeover Episodes 1-4